The Ground Is Full of Holes

The Ground Is Full of Holes

Suzy Norman

Patrician Press

Manningtree

First published as a paperback edition by Patrician Press 2019

British Library Cataloguing in Publication Data. A catalogue record for this book is available from the British Library.

ISBN paperback edition 978-1-9997030-4-2

Published by Patrician Press 2019

For my parents

Sometimes the soul takes pictures of things it has wished for, but never seen.

Ann Sexton

They had been so compatible, he always felt. It's a long life, his mother Shelagh had warned him one afternoon at the breakfast table, you have to make sure you marry the right person. Well, he was sure. Everyone lives for love. Colleagues who worked with him at the hospital were unlikely to think of him – a high-flying anaesthetist with an unblemished reputation – a romantic. But he knows he is a romantic, in the sense he believes in a one, true love and that love is worth risking everything for. What happens when two people marry is rarely straight-forward, Shelagh had warned him, often a series of events, consecutive, but not always related, build and build until a situation – another type of situation, a complicated one – races away with its own momentum, but at this point, he'd stopped listening. He'd had his mind on other things.

He stops to breathe for just a moment. The air hangs around him, hotter than the motionless air in theatre, deep in the bowels of the hospital. What is that, he thinks, feather-light, so light as to not be there at all?

1

He feels the pull of it, as if it were a magnetic strip. Once again he's overcome with a sense of unreality, unsettling, expanding all. The air changes, darkens, as it always does when it's around. He watches her blink and her black, inquisitive eyes. It is as if her eyes are his own; he recognises the loneliness in them. She looks into his blue eyes – bluer than the Mediterranean sea his wife had told him, staring out to sea during their last holiday in Menorca. He'd often wondered what Asabi saw when she looked at him.

Earlier, in front of the mirror, he'd tried to see his eyes as he imagines Asabi surely sees them. He had tried to picture them as warm and seductive – irresistible even – but this morning he'd only seen empty shells.

What? Asabi asks.

Her lips move. He watches them. They seem to vibrate and he wants to shake her in the empty, sterile corridor, with the stench of industrial bleach.

Christ, he says, the expectation in them, your warm brown pools.

What do you mean, Marcus?

He taps the corner of her essay and pulls the papers from her hand.

Okay then, he says, you know how it is, I'll get back to you when I can.

When exactly?

Bold of you to ask, he says. What makes you think you can ask me that? What level of intimacy do you think we're working under, exactly?

She smiles and he smiles too. He looks down at the over-sized, manly face of the watch his mother had bought him as a birthday present. He hated it. There is a rush of tiles at his feet as he advances away.

In many ways he wishes it was some years in the future, ten or eleven should suffice. Enough time to have flowed through the murky rivers of his mind would mean there was some distance, he could enjoy her, the memory of her, a revenant. Being face to face with her every day at work could make his heart stop sometimes. It made his breath quicken, his body sweat. Not in a way he enjoyed, and not always in a sexual way, a guilty way, gloomy and dark. If his emotional entanglement with her was far enough in the past he could relax, maybe even sit back and smile when he thinks of her, what they'd managed to get away with. He suspects it will happen one day, but not yet. He'd have the memory to keep him warm, and he knew that was all anyone could ask from life.

She hadn't been the first. No, Asabi had been the second, chronologically and also, if he was honest with himself, in status. The first time he'd betrayed Nancy had been extraordinary, meant something but he often wondered if that was true, or that his heart had been softer then. Perhaps her greatest legacy, the first betrayal, had been not that she had stolen his heart but she'd pulled open his jacket, pushed her hand in his chest and replaced his heart with one she'd sculpted out of Irish clay. Few people had the power to do this to another human being. Human folly was to seek them out only to play out the story.

He'd boarded a flight back to Dublin, an impulse. It's just work had been hell, closed off and mute. London was the hottest he could remember it being, neighbours, voluminous like never before, car horns, demented – hell, hell, all around. At least Ireland was quiet and familiar. Not that he cared about that; he just needed a change of scene. Through the windows on the plane home he'd seen lightening and soupy clouds. As soon as the taxi dropped him off in town, he boarded the first DART over to Dún Laoghaire.

Standing on the stone wall as the sun was going down, the rain far off but the promise of it in the skies England way, his heart beat deep inside his body. Feeling as distant as the rain England way, heading over slowly, he breathed in the salty air as it clung to the fibres of his lungs, but he didn't care, this is what he wanted. He missed the sea. It was a physical need to be close to to the sea, of this he was sure.

It was then he saw her, not a moment you can easily forget and yet not picture-perfect either. What he had come to realise was this: you can feel pity for someone and admiration in the same moment. He missed the mystery of sizing up a new woman, admiring her wide hips, delighting in the way nature cleverly designs a woman. He missed losing himself in a woman's eyes, and wondering if her baby would have his glacial eyes or hers – or an amalgam of the two. It was a game he enjoyed playing, and it gave excitement to any new encounter.

She moved towards him in Dún Laoghaire, slowly as if the weight of her right hip was too heavy to carry her. It was a lopsided walk, no two ways about that. There had been something about the way she determined, a certain grace to the way she approached – grace, yes, he'd often thought that.

Chris, his colleague, brushes past him and a hand slaps his back.

Alright, Marcus? How is it with you, sir? How is it with you, man?

A nurse passes in creased cotton. He feels a flash of desire. This too fades. From the front desk in his department, unmanned again for the third time this week, he grabs his list for the day and clutches it tight to his chest.

His thoughts return to his quiet wife at home. He can't remember when it was she'd stopped speaking to him, a mystery. He is sure that her long silence was somehow down to a fault of his own. She was, in some small way, an embodiment of all his childhood desires. She was dark and full-bodied like those children's presenters he lusted after as a kid. His ideal one-day wife would be Sally James, or as near an approximation as possible. Shapely, homely, with just a hint of spike.

Fortunately, the quarter moon appeared behind her. If it had been a full moon he might have gazed at it a beat too long and missed her entirely. Silence descended. The sound of kids complaining they were cold, hungry, bored, and so on, fell away. Tiny hands carrying buckets and spades faded into the distance. Even the retreating ferry seemed to shut off the engine and glide. The water was oily and unpleasant, but the salt in his lungs pleased him. Her mouth was open, just a touch, her eyes closed against the wind, blowing up as if from nowhere. He glanced furtively over his shoulder, as if someone he knew might be watching them, his eyes fixed on his target, this perfect, imperfect stranger.

In theatre, every pair of eyes is fixed on the body on the slab. He looks down to his hands, pale and inured to the artificial light in the rancid, felching bowel of the building. William, the surgeon turns to face him.

As I've said before, the safety briefing is *extremely* important. Lateness simply won't be tolerated.

Marcus wants to laugh and he wonders what would happen if he did actually laugh in front of all these people.

Lateness simply won't be tolerated, William says again.

A new face with coral cheeks introduces herself to the group. He watches her hair float around in the blank, white space. Her peroxide hair, a cone of hay, seems to buzz under the strip light. He is afraid for her. Patiently he waits. William hands her a bucket and asks her to collect gas from the ward needed for the procedure. She takes it from him and cheerily announces she'll be back in a minute. Some of the others swallow down a cough. A couple of the others laugh.

William scans the room until his eyes land on Marcus and then gently lifts the head of the pensioner on the slab. There is a strange, old man smell. Marcus tries to keep down a wave of acid reflux, staring at the orange wax in the pensioner's ears.

Second is a lap anterior resection, William says, I also need to do a sigmoidoscopy. I start these in right lateral to mobilise the splenic flexure, then supine with legs up.

When he's finished, William stretches his arms wide and smiles.

If that's okay with you, doctor, he says to Marcus.

Marcus nods.

I'll use the harmonic scalpel, William says. Usual antibiotics. Anything else?

No, he's a fit and well sixty-five year old, Marcus says. No anaesthetic issues.

Marcus turns to Lana, the Romanian assistant, wiry and blonde. He might have fancied her once, but he'd since concluded she was the kind of person you could easily forget.

I'll have a big Fentanyl now, thanks, Marcus says to her.

Lana turns her back and he watches her move until she becomes a blur of light and pixels. She moves fast, he thinks, unlike his wife these days. What he wouldn't give to see his wife move fast for a change. Lana liked to please him. He wishes there were a few more like her around these days.

As Lana scrambles among the implements on the trolley, the coral-cheeked nurse returns clutching her bucket. William takes it from her.

You're lucky, she says, they told me on the ward it's all they had left.

The room explodes with laughter and the sound still

crackles in his head when he finds himself alone in the monitor room. He knows he's done everything right because he's done it all a thousand times before. When Asabi wafts in and stands beside him, he wants to say this: Your eyes, in me, outside of me, but in me. There's no space between us, never has been. He wants to say this, but instead he says nothing.

He thought it was important to remain calm and listen to her. She'd had multiple sclerosis all her life, she told him, she'd already lived longer than anyone had expected. Rain descended so quickly the others in the café stopped eating and stared at the steam spreading across the windows. Struggling against the wind down at the harbour, he'd offered her his arm. By accepting his aid, he witnessed a beauty, vulnerability and strength he couldn't recall having seen before, even in his capacity of doctor. Her name, she told him, was Kim.

The rain stopped as quickly as it appeared. The sun streaked through the pane, drawing out the red tones in her dark hair. At times, he said, he felt it so intensely, he missed home. His candour was a shock even to himself. He'd said he'd often fantasised about moving back without his wife, without his profession, try another kind a life, a better kind of life. He had an English name because his mother had been ambitious and had in fact followed him to London as soon as he became a student. But he missed Dublin. Immediately he felt lighter telling her all this. What he didn't say was he often felt he belonged in Dublin, not in London in a sea of blank faces.

She never used to have baths like these, she used to prefer showers and she'd be quick too, enjoying the sharp needles, the pressure drawing her back to life. All the shit, the dirt, the hurt, she used to tell herself. A dab of lime gel to get the blood pumping. Need to be wide awake for a day of screwing over the rich – paper pushing, wheedling, manipulating, the Goddess of all things money, honey. Now though, she'd rather wallow. She lifts her foot out from her coconut and lychee bubbles and sighs. She'd learned from her own mother, Julia, that love must be something you work at, and when disconnection occurs, you just paddle harder, faster. Yes, it goes without saying, with the man you already have.

Last week, her father-in-law Frank had fitted gold taps for her. She couldn't remember now if she'd asked him to fit them, or just sadly pointed at them stacked next to the fitted wardrobe in the spare room. One of the unexpected fall-outs of sadness, she'd learned was redecorating.

She pulls out the bath plug. As she does so, she imagines the small hole has the power to suck away a wave of grief, but if she was honest with herself the grief had started long before she had met Marcus. He'd crashed into her life. The letters of his name often circle in her mind, morphing into a life of their own. Dark blue, always blue.

She closes her eyes and wonders where Marcus ends and she begins. Her breath tightens again. Last night she'd complained to her best friend, Anna, who had patiently listened without interruption. She is forty-four and yet struggles to remember the last time she met somebody new. When was the last new person, male or female? She had concluded on the spot there were less opportunities to meet people these days. The loss of possibilities had dawned on her so slowly she had hardly noticed but now it pained her to think about it all. Having exciting experiences, even travelling to new places, was a distant memory.

Their last holiday, Menorca had been a disaster. A chance to bring them closer together in neutral territory had only pulled them apart. With nowhere left to go on the island, they sat together on their tiny balcony. Marcus hated it. A door with a baby gate, he'd said. But these places were always smaller than they looked online, she'd reminded him. They'd spent a long evening smoking cheap menthols, staring out to sea and after three hours the hills began to move in on them. For her, the plane journey back to Gatwick could not have come soon enough.

She looks down to a mound of flab protruding from the water and brushes her fingertips along her stomach. The bank emailed her regularly to ask if she was okay. When will you be back, Squid, they asked her only last week. Soon, but not yet, she'd told them, first there were matters at home to deal with. She can't remember why she was known as Squid, but she'd grown to like it all the more for there not being any real story behind it. For a second, she wonders what the world would be like without stories – no history, no prehistory, no judgements on behaviour. She couldn't image it, but she imagines it would feel nice for a change.

The night she first met Marcus had been the night Anna her best friend had introduced her to the pubs of Bethnal Green. She remembers the fag-stained wallpaper and stench of smoke on the curtains. Bethnal Green had been a novelty then, a grimy little urban village, an alternative to the quiet, smart pubs of West London. Nobody else she knew went there.

It had been October, late in the evening. She remembers above all else his jacket with the tiny squares. A padded jacket with the zip broken half-way down

She watched him burst in from the rain, noting the angry way he pulled the sleeve of his jacket from his arm. She looked closer at his long, slender fingers, tense and clawed. She had wanted to soothe him, clutch him to her. She'd risked a nervous glance at Anna, as if Anna could save her from herself, as if Anna had all the answers. But Anna was in no position to help.

She sighs and looks around the bathroom. The enamel on the sink is chipped. Another thing she's forgotten to fix. In an effort to feel herself again, she'd hatched a plan with Anna to transform the house. She'd ordered candles for around the fireplace, tall and thick that would take a lifetime to burn down to the wick. She wanted a new dark wood floor and a new white ceiling to sit back and stare mindlessly at. Wherever she saw an opportunity for improvement, she could cling to some hope for a happier future. There were to be flecks of gold in the bedroom and burnt orange cushions on the bed.

She'd told Marcus she'd wanted a new sound about the house. This is bullshit, he'd said in response. A new what? What part of your brain tells you that I want to stare at orange all day? You're always thinking you can do what you want and I'll just play along. Worse still, you actually think this *means* something. This childish, displacement crap you're into, it won't wash.

She'd kept to her plan. Not everything needed to change, she told him to try and soften him. They could keep the bathroom just past the kitchen, just how Marcus's Granny used to have it over in Ireland that time they visited together. This, at least, seemed to appease him. There had been something about that small town with its red painted doors that had transfixed her. She saw endless sands and a rough sea with thorny edges that stretched, she imagined, all the way to Belfast.

In Anna's company, she returned to her obsession with the house. She'd keep the outdoor toilet for emergencies. The weeds growing in the stone floor gave the small space character, she told Anna, and besides it was another chance for Marcus to rile their neighbour, Blake. Blake had crushed his beer can in his hand when Marcus bust out of there, zipping his fly that time. Anything to get Blake going.

Nancy steps out of the bath, dresses herself in the dark, empty hall – empty except for a piano she rarely touched these days. She pulls on her beige brogue boots, scuffed at the tip. Slowly, she fastens the laces. Today she decides, she'll walk to the furthest bakery. She hasn't left the house for days.

Nancy opens the front door. Looking down to a small heap of envelopes by her feet, one in particular stands out. Recognising the handwriting as Georgia's, she peels back the flap of the envelope. There is a picture of a teddy bear resting in a rocking chair.

Here's hoping. Just to let you know, Shiv and I are thinking of you both. Love you xx

Her shaking hand holds it tight. Last week she regretted telling Georgia her news. There had been a time when they were able to keep everything a secret, Marcus and her, living in their own world.

Three months after Nancy and Marcus had first met, they'd spent three carefree weeks travelling around the Golden Triangle. It had been easy to walk around in a bikini top and mini skirt, unaware her life and body would one day change forever, yet everything changed when they landed back on British soil. A full table of friends down the pub had been replaced with empty seats – or else there were swollen bumps endlessly multiplying. Her friends' questions had stung. When was it going to be her turn? You can't keep putting babies off forever.

Nancy buttons up her cord blazer and steps out onto the stone step. Marcus had resisted the attentions of the women she was convinced tried so hard to take him away from her. She knew he was the best looking doctor in the hospital. Most of all, she feared the nurses, the ones who were looking for a doctor as a route to a family and a big house in the country. She thinks again of Marcus and the first night they met, how seeing him made her feel inside.

The shouting voices in the pub fell silent. Turning to face her at the bar, he'd smiled, breaking his stern expression for her. It had been Halloween. On the bar, a pumpkin shone, a mouth curled and judging. There had been a rustle of paper. A woman with whitened face and thick ghoulish eye-liner had dropped a pound in the jukebox. Something from the sixties, she was sure, although she couldn't remember the song, lots of yeahs and oohs. Marcus had leaned in to her, smelling of warm hops. He'd just started work for Bart's Trust, he'd said.

There had been a tightness in her chest, making her want to laugh. He leaned in close and she'd smiled nervously. There had been something behind his half-grin that both made her afraid and drew her in. He'd glanced down to her kitten heels and shrugged at her question. Nervously, afraid to fall too hard too fast, she'd kept her gaze low on his dark blue jeans, noting the casual way they hung around his hips. She wondered had he lost weight.

The clouds above her head turn the colour of the wet slate roofs. She pulls open her umbrella and turns into the Fulham Road. Though the road is familiar to her, it looks longer under the blanket of the sky. She walks on, pushing her hands deep in her blazer pockets. When she reaches the sewing shop, she stops. In the window are burnt, terracotta pots piled high with wool. A woman sips tea behind the till. Nancy watches her mouth purse against the steam.

The following day, Anna had nagged her to email him. Instead, Nancy tried to distract herself at the gym by pounding on the treadmill, but her mind kept returning to him. She knew she would see him again, it was just a case of when.

The wind bares its teeth. The tube draws near. She speeds up, thinking ahead to later, to their next counselling session in Liverpool Street. Poor, sweet June, she thinks, up against Marcus's intractable silence. She calculates it will be under an hour until she sees her in the usual small room in Liverpool Street.

A sharp pain spears her foot. The culprit, a pair of mustard stilettos move down the quiet street. She glances at her watch. Strange to think she was still with Shiv when she met Marcus.

She knows now she needn't have worried. There was one incident in particular which confirmed what she long suspected about Shiv's feelings for Georgia, forever branded in her mind as the umbrella incident. The sky had turned to mud. A groan filled the air, a warning of a storm coming. Shiv pulled away from Nancy in the hall, ran to the door, and with his black umbrella opened wide, he ran down the drive to Georgia.

Marcus takes a moment in his office. With Chris gone, he pulls out a chair, leans back and stares up at the ceiling. He couldn't face seeing June again, not after the last session he'd attended alone. It had felt wrong, sitting across from her in that poky room, her smile warm and her eyes expecting him to smile back.

Fair to say she was everything I could hope to find, he tells her, and I was beginning to think I never would.

Really? Go on.

Why do you do that?

I'm sorry?

Tension rises through his body, his neck feels stiff and he rubs it a little. June waits for him to continue.

When I'm about to say something, you narrow your eyes. I'm not sure I like it, it looks a little sarcastic. Are you really interested? Because I'm wondering, when am I going to say something you're satisfied with, that'll pull you back from staring at the damn clock? Have I not said anything of interest to you – real interest – in all the weeks I've been coming here?

I don't think that I…

I'm sorry, he says sighing. Suddenly the room is too small and he wants to go

I'm just thinking back, he says, some of it is a blur if I'm honest. Nancy was after flirting with me. I was tired, tired after that damn operation, I've told you before about it, I'm sure. The operation with the wrong arm – but that wasn't me, that was Will. I wouldn't make a stupid mistake like that. Blatant flirting. She was trying to be coy but I saw through it. God, I wanted her instantly, fucking instantly. What is it now? What? I could tell by the way your eyes closed that you didn't like it. I – Oh, it doesn't matter. But I'm expressing myself and that's important, why I'm here, isn't it? Look, I don't mean to sound so direct, but I need to remind myself sometimes, how sleek and fine she looked. It was one of those blank, slightly innocuous faces. And no, before you say it, I don't know what that means either. I couldn't hear her and I wanted to. Softly spoken in a noisy pub on Halloween. Smoky, noisy, the kind of place I'm used to, but it didn't seem her sort of place. Well, you've unlocked something in me, I've only just remembered it was Halloween. Sorry, you don't think it's funny? Maybe it was a full moon too because I was fierce with desire. Thing is, I don't know what else to say about that first meeting, what else is there to say? Irritating, isn't it? Her friend seemed to like me, those green eyes of her burning into my soul. She was cute but I didn't like the way she walked. Stomping around in those heels so everyone would turn around and look at her. Attention seeking behaviour. Hate it. Not like my wife, quiet and the type of person you wanted to know because of it. What? You think I'm embellishing, flattering myself? A man notices these things. He *always* notices these things.

When the session is over and June asks him if he wants to come alone again another time, he hesitates for a moment. A small, damp patch in the corner of the ceiling becomes the object of his focus. He feels like he's been remanded in a cell for the past hour.

No, I don't think that's necessary, he says.

He gets up out of his chair and hovers for a moment. The light through the vertical blinds creates stripes on his chest. He's at least relieved it's going to be a rain-free day. Chris will be returning soon and he has to move. Earlier, over breakfast, he'd regretted what he'd said to June. It had been unfair on Nancy, a lukewarm account of that first meeting and not a true reflection of his feeling at all. The truth was he'd felt drawn to her as if unexpectedly. Without fully knowing, he'd found himself a reason to be alive. As he grabs the office door handle, he decides he needs a holiday and soon.

Kim was staying at The Morgan hotel, she told him. She had to get away from her mother for the night. For the most part, they got on well, but it was an act of kindness, giving her space for the night. But there was another reason for her visit, a more important one. She had an open day to attend at Trinity the following day. She was planning to apply to study English Literature and she was hopeful for a scholarship. Would he come with her?

Burnt orange and sienna lines, loosely woven protect her from the cold breeze floating through the window. She wriggles her bare legs further up under her blanket. Warming herself this way she tries to calm her thoughts.

Marcus stands by the window looking out at the grey sky. She swallows hard to see him silent, not offering, not trying to resolve. As she watches him, she wonders what he'd look like lying on a slab like one of his patients, anaesthetised, covered in blood, being pulled apart by a surgeon. She wants to laugh.

Marcus looks down to see a drop of blood on his hand – a drop of blood where her nails had swiped seconds before. His right foot faces her, but the left foot points towards the door. In just under an hour he will be due back at the hospital. Watching him breathe, the floor shifts, or she thinks it does, certainty bends. She presses her toes down onto the dark wood panels and lets out a slow moan. Marcus opens his mouth and closes it again. He flexes his arms in the air and stretches his fingers up towards the ceiling.

Yeah, he says, well I kind of liked that phone.

That's it, she says, that's all you're going to say?

What else is there to say?

Her back aches from slouching. She looks out of the window and sees the sky is striped blue again. A feeling of gloom takes her over, making her head spin. She senses the night ahead is going to be long.

Leaving the window, he comes over to her and sits by her side. She knows he wants to be away from her, battling the crowds on his way to work, heading to Bart's, anywhere else. She studies his neutral face and fights an urge to want to touch him. He perches forward on the sofa and peers into a basket on the floor. There is a ball of crimson wool and knitting needles stab the fibrous aorta.

If you can't stop, he says, you're going to have to leave this house. Because it's mine and it's best you understand this now before it's too late. You hit me. You're making me point this out to you, aren't you?

His hand brushes her hair. She pushes his hand away. He sits back in his navy jogging pants. An hour earlier, his parents had called around. Disastrous timing, she'd hissed at him as Shelagh and Frank had rang the doorbell over and over again. Sensing the icy chill in the air, and up against Marcus's stubborn wall of silence, Frank had thrown Shelagh a look. Peter Jones will be closing soon, they'd said, best get a move on.

A door clicks. Rising slowly to her feet, she goes to the window and watches him, a face cocooned under a charcoal hood. Light rain begins to fall, dancing under the street lights. There is nothing for her to do but wait. Minutes pass. Maybe an hour. She's not sure.

June drags her bloated, fluid-filled ankles into the tiny reception room where Nancy waits next to a grime-splattered window she's been staring out of for the past ten minutes. June's body, Nancy thinks, reflects her professionalism, her dedication to psychotherapy. A woman who patiently listens, she imagines, would accrue calories as easily as others offload. To their right, the receptionist stirs her coffee behind a desk, frowning, concentrating on the computer screen. Nancy wonders what could be so important and troubling. She's forgotten what being at work involves.

I haven't had many, Nancy begins after they've settled into

their chairs in the consultancy room. Men, I mean, not as many as my friends have had, I'm sure.

How many?

One or two, maybe. I haven't really thought about it much. I brought a boy home once.

A long time ago? How old were you?

Sixteen, maybe. No, seventeen. He was older, at least I think that's right. He wasn't a serious boyfriend but I liked him a lot. No, alright, the truth, I liked him, *liked* him. In fact, I dumped Ed for him. I think it was his hair, long, curly and thick, just my type. But when Ed found out, well we – that's Julia, my mother and me – we watched him drive past the window. It was funny. He used to drive a Mini Cooper, but he was so tall and it was so funny to see him angry like that, driving past with his knees up to his chin. Julia said, a cuckold, if ever I saw one. We laughed together, Mum and me. Of course, it *was* funny, him in that tiny car with those daddy-long-legs of his. So, Tom. Well…I brought him home the next day. But Julia, my mother, she just glared at him.

Okay, June says, smiling. So, what happened to Tom?

I'm not sure. Well, I – what I mean is there was just that letter.

June puts the lid back on her pen and fondles the large, wooden beads on her necklace.

A letter?

He wrote to me from his halls in Oxford. He told me all about the little things he liked to do to help him cope with being away. It was so… so tender. He told me about his new alarm clock. He told me all about his tiny room, every last detail. There was just this cupboard for his clothes and a small sink above his bed. Handy for a late night piss, he said. Oh… and the posters he was choosing. I can't now remember which ones. Marley smoking a giant spliff, probably. Or The Blues Brothers, any one of the student clichés? I don't know. He missed me, but if he sat down with a cup of tea he could cope. Quite honestly? I don't know why I'm telling you all this. He wrote me a letter. There was just that one but I don't think I replied. It's possible, I suppose, but I don't think so, it's too long ago. Do you think this…? I don't know why – why this is in my mind today? It was so long ago. Everything was different back then. Life stretched ahead of us. I suppose it was a bit like… well, I don't know, like life was a roll of tissue paper or something. I'm thinking of the Andrex puppy in that advert, dragging paper down the hall – long, so very long. No, I can't say why I'm – because in all honesty, I haven't thought of him in twenty years. You do believe me, don't you?

June taps her pen against the notepad resting on her lap and glances at the door. Nancy knows by this gesture, that the session is at an end until next time.

Experimentally, he tilts his plate. Two eggs excrete a light film of grease and he watches them slide towards the edge of the plate. Two months into his experiment in vegetarianism, and he wonders if he can go on.

The canteen staff viewed his kind with suspicion, militant

in his demand for a meal other than faggots and lumpen mashed potato. His favourite, a Polish woman moves behind the counter. He watches her ladle her soup with Zeppelin arms.

Peering down at his laptop, he scans the words that comprise his research notes. He knows he needs to sharpen his opener, make it less vague. He thinks after his scheduled operation, if all goes to plan, he can do so then. Mindlessly, he stabs a chip and chews it slowly.

On the wooden floor somewhere near him, a chair squeaks. He doesn't look up but he knows from the way the air changes, darkens, that it's Asabi. There is a tightly bound silence before she opens her mouth. He watches her slide into frame, unsmiling, her eyes staring down to his research notes on gastrointestinal complications. He thinks when she sighs, she sounds like a cat sighing, aware of it's own power.

Eating alone again, doctor? She asks. This is becoming a regular occurrence.

Smiling, she pulls out a chair. He imagines her drifting in and out of the circles of her own thoughts, in and out of his own. He tries to remember when he first started to find her desirable. The previous Christmas he'd offered to read her essays. It had been a chance to be close to her skin, clear and smooth, like brown sugar drizzled on warm cake. The truth was he'd taken pity on her. He was sure last year when he'd taken her under his wing, his intentions had been no more than paternal. She was young, in need of him, watched and judged as she was under the microscope. Everyone was watched closely in the hospital, especially a new girl.

So, have you read it? She asks.

Read what?

Don't be funny, Marcus. The essay. Was it coherent? Was it okay?

She leans her head back, flashing her eyes up to the ceiling. They seem to empty. This unnerves him. Slowly she blows her lips.

You're certainly theatrical, he says.

She ignores this, and with a gesture he normally reserves for his patients, Marcus taps her hand. He is once again surprised by how light and bony she feels. He pushes his half-drunk coffee to one side, clearing a path between them.

You haven't read it, have you? She says.

Honestly? I haven't had the time. I'm sorry.

He taps his pager on the table. Taking a cue from this, Asabi slinks out of the wooden chair. The ceiling appears to lower and darken to match her eyes.

Okay, so, she says. I suppose you're busy again.

Look, he says, the truth is I'm far too busy. That can't come as a surprise to you, can it? No, don't hang your head like that. Don't you – don't *you* look at me the same way the others do.

What do you mean, Marcus?

Nothing.

Don't be getting paranoid now, she says. But thank you, Dr Connell, for your time.

After she's gone and a safe minute or two has passed, he pounds the empty corridors. He thinks about the day ahead. Tolerance and patience were virtues he needed in the hospital, but lately he wasn't sure he had any. The wiry, Romanian nurse passes him, her head down. A familiar face approaches. Walsh taps Marcus lightly on the shoulder.

He had never met anyone else like him in the profession. Walsh was the man everyone wanted to be. The media hung on his every word when they wanted clarification on a new health development. His quotes appeared regularly in the nationals. Patients' condemned faces were brighter and restored after leaving his consultancy room. For Marcus, it was absurd to think anyone was above him in the pecking order at the hospital, but the hospital was a complex and confusing organ. Wielding budgets as weapons, the management consultants held the power.

Are they ready yet? Walsh asks him. Don't look at me dumb man. The same notes you're holding in your hands.

After Marcus has delivered his patter of excuses, Walsh's heavy footsteps move on in the direction of oncology. Another doctor brushes past him. Their arms touch but neither apologises. He feels sure he recognises the face and wonders if he may have worked with him once, one of the competitive, bloated types, a few more of them around these days.

His thoughts return to Asabi and the obvious contempt in her eyes. He could take her somewhere, away from all all they knew, The Malsaison Oxford, maybe, a former prison. He thinks of her sweet, moist lips and her eyes, quarter moons. The bend of her back against the drugs trolley.

He was sure Asabi wanted to close the gap between them every bit as much as he wanted to. He also suspected she put him on a pedestal, had illusions of him being some kind of a martyr. During his last shift, thinking about her smile that never fully committed, he'd thought of his drug of choice, Propofol. He could take just enough to numb the pain. Damage limitation would be all.

She had been wet, wetter than he could ever remember any woman being. A wild cat, all tears and gratitude. Slipping through his fingers, he'd turned her into nothing more than a torn sheet on the floor. Two breaths later, she had been a great shark, dipping and diving through the linen. She'd been a hot-breathed devil pressing down on his chest; a cruel, selfish spider clamped around his leg. Those quarter moon eyes had sunk down into his soul. He could have become addicted.

Afterwards, when she was dressed again she'd reached into her bag for her keys. He'd experienced a crushing low he could only approximate with drug withdrawal. It was as if he and the stars were one, and the feeling terrified him. It was a feeling of unreality, of wanting to rip open the universe and find a new one, one where there was a definite ceiling between him and the stars.

Kim asked him up for a coffee and he agreed. His over-riding need was to stay close to her, to somehow find a way to keep talking. In her room on the second floor, he sat at her writing desk with his back to her while she lay back on the bed. At that moment, he was afraid to turn around, to make the next move, but he had to be near her somehow.

Somehow the minutes passed. He rose out of his chair and went into the bathroom. A make-up bag overflowed, cotton wool pads, a pink lipstick – had she been wearing any? He didn't think so. A tampon, nail varnish remover, a hair comb, a few strays of her dark hair in the sink by the plug. The enamel was chipped near the tap. All he could think was she deserved better. This enraged him so much he wanted to call down to reception and demand an upgrade for her free of charge. What was happening to Dublin? Money grabbing, but no care, no care.

Are you coming back to me, he heard her say. She sounded faint as if she was in another room entirely.

In a minute, he said.

He heard shrieking and laughing, too loud and raucous to be anything less than a hen party. The noise passed their room and then faded. How long until the next one disturbed their peace, he wondered. His mouth was dry and he upturned her toothbrush and placed the glass under the tap. As he drank, he looked at his face in the mirror. Strange how artificial light could make a face seem drier and older, he thought, as if hotel bathrooms all over the world only existed to play cruel tricks.

He headed back into the room where she was sitting at the desk, rifling through the hotel notepad he'd drawn on.

You draw very badly, she said. Are we after going out? I'm not sure I want to be here now.

What she did next surprised him. She threw the pad over her shoulder and it crashed on the side of the wall-mounted television. She moved across to his feet and untied his trainers. As he sat on the edge of the bed, she removed them, slowly, carefully.

You're not very good at taking a hint either, she said.

With his mind focused again, he kicks open the door to theatre and he is relieved to see it is just him and the blonde Romanian scrub nurse. Shyly, she points to the list on the wall.

What is on with this afternoon, doctor?

Effortlessly, Marcus decodes her broken English.

A craniopathy. All being well, but it's no concern of mine, I'm not on duty tonight.

She bends down to pick up a dropped scalpel. Marcus watches her wrap the scalpal in a tissue. Idly, he eyes the locked drugs cabinet behind her. 3-5mls of propofol, just to ease the burden, enough to make him drowsy.

Lana taps his shoulder. Her fingers are syringes, taunting him.

Oh, but I thought? Okay, doctor. So, I can go now?

He waves to the door and when she's gone, he fingers the lock on the drugs cupboard. He imagines grabbing Asabi's legs and pulling them apart, clamping the palm of this hand around her tiny waist.

Opening the grey metal door of the cupboard, he puts his hand inside. He knows if he is caught taking volatile anaesthetics it will be the end of his career. No doubt about it.

The swirled, Islamic tile under her foot is still cracked. She slams the door behind her and takes a deep breath. A van screeches to a halt and a large, iron crate falls from the back. The sound overtakes her and makes her want to retreat inside. When she is feeling brave again, she takes another deep breath and puts her foot forward. As she leaves the front drive, she thinks ahead to later. She is sure she'll be unable to order her words and make herself understood. Julia, her mother, had been even more sceptical than Marcus, told her therapy was an expensive waste of time.

It's unnatural, all that naval gazing, Julia had said. Look at the Catholics! Out-and-out weirdos. I suppose they think if they confess all, they can behave exactly how they like? Well, you know what I'm getting at, don't you?

Upstairs in the consultancy room that is no bigger than Nancy's box room, with the same magnolia paint, Nancy's thoughts simmer. She watches June cross her inflated ankles.

Now, so…

Yes? Nancy asks.

So, you left a message with reception saying Marcus

29

couldn't make it, but that was fine because this time you wanted to come by yourself.

Nancy nods, soothed to hear her telephone conversation relayed back to her like this. She remembers, yes, she had definitely said to the receptionist she had wanted to come alone.

But sometimes these sessions are the most useful ones, June says. Enjoyable, even.

Are memories reliable, June?

Explain?

Only I've been thinking, why did we feel a need to invest so much hope into our marriage? Our small, calm house… at least I think it's calm… at least it is most of the time, it's certainly small, but I'm sure I'd wanted to drive a wedge between us. Did I even stop to think about this at all?

A comforting smell of coffee from the bakery below wafts in. Nancy breathes in slowly and bends down to tie the ribbons on her purple pumps. June waits, but all Nancy can think of is how unfair it is a consultant doctor who earns as much as Marcus can only afford a two-bedroom terrace in Fulham. She has never shared her disappointment with June, believing June to have even less to show for a lifetime of work.

Look, Nancy says, I know we haven't been for a while, but well – alright, I'm useless, I can't make a decision for myself. I'm useless.

June listens and shakes her head. Her eyes remind Nancy

of sidelights on a car in the fog, misty with concern. Nancy reclines further back into the sponge chair.

I'm a big kid, Nancy says. Do you agree?

Well, no, actually…

It's like I'm a child – a child learning to take small steps again. Learning to listen. And sex. Oh God, don't even get me started on that. It's like I'm learning to try and enjoy sex again. The tiring rigmarole of it, the disconnect between us. How can I even think about sex when it's an effort to even get out of bed? Having to remember to wrap up warm now the weather's turned. Too many things.

And Marcus? June asks. How is Marcus?

Oh, Nancy says. Sometimes it's like I buckle under the weight. The pressure, it's like I'm learning to – learning to speak to my sister on the phone again. I'm forty fucking four for Christ's sake and it's like, I'm just learning to start again. I only have… words. And I have to somehow get the few words I want to say out in the right order. I'm a sedated animal, that's what I am. I'm a fucking elephant peering through the railings. An elephant with big, stupid – yes, yes, big stupid eyes.

June taps her finger on the tip of her biro.

And how long have you been feeling like this?

Nancy shrugs.

I'm trying to drink water, Nancy says. More water but I don't like the taste. Evian tastes like nothing. Volvic tastes like metal. Anna – that's my friend. She thinks I should drink more water, that's all.

That's all? June asks.

Nancy wants to stare out of the window and say nothing more. There are patches of green mildew around the edge of the pane. A fly thrashes against the glass.

I know how you feel, fly.

Sorry? June asks.

D, Nancy says. The letter D, that's all. Now look, I can't think with you staring at me like that. Disappointment, disillusionment, depletion, defeat. No, none of these! Devastation. Devastated! So, this is why counselling is useful, mother.

Nancy watches June clasp her hands together.

Anna, June says, so remind me, is this your friend whose husband walked out?

Anna? Yes, she went crazy for a while, started stealing. So stupid, I told her. I told her you'll be caught in the end, that's what happens to everyone if they keep on doing it. It was only small things at first, loo rolls from café toilets, ashtrays… from pubs, that type of thing, but then she got bold, sandwiches from the supermarket. She'd eat them while she was walking around but discard the wrapper so she wouldn't have to pay. Of course it escalated from there, these things always do. A lipstick from Primark – Primark! Here's what I think of your lipstick, she must have told herself and slipped it in her pocket. Fuck capitalism, June?

June waits.

She fancied herself as a new person, Nancy says. A guerrilla shopper, but she was just a thief. She stopped when she was caught, of course, had to then. And I was right, she *did* get caught. They bundled her in a back room. Short shrift from the security staff seemed to work. Anyway... I'm going on too much. You can tell me to stop if you like, or try to steer me onto another topic of conversation, I don't mind, I'm open to suggestion.

No, June says.

She's stopped asking me how I'm feeling, Nancy says.

Who? Anna?

Can't blame her, Nancy says. She's not the only one who's stopped asking.

June tries not to clench her hands. She rests her elbows on the arms of her chair.

Shelagh though, that's Marcus's mother. I know she wants to ask but somehow she never manages to. Scared of the answer, I suppose. Take last week: they called over unannounced, all the way from Kingston. A freezing cold day. On and on she went. Yakked endlessly about her Fortnum's tea and her crystallised bloody kumquats. Then it was the serious-concerned face and that beautiful, soft Irish accent of hers probing me. Can I offer you another lime cream, Nancy? But she didn't care if I answered or not, her type never do. It was hopeless. She just sat there looking at my sad eyes. Sad elephant eyes.

Tell me more about the elephant, June says. I'm intrigued by her, this elephant.

Well, elephants mourn their dead, don't they? They *acknowledge* death, at least. They scan their trunks over the carcass of relatives, like huge bar code detectors. Oh, I don't – but they're registering, aren't they? Processing their grief.

I suppose so, June says. A smart analogy, if that's how you see yourself.

I'm not smart.

To say they feel emotion is stretching it a bit, June says, but there's a process, yes, a process of meditation before rejoining the herd. Only then they carry on with their lives?

Maybe, Nancy says.

June relaxes her hands and rests her palms flat on her knees. Finally, she glances up at the clock on the wall.

But nobody's died, Nancy.

I know, but my father died, and I thought I'd be over it by now. I need to slow down and order my thinking. Okay, forget the stupid elephants. Time is money, right? At least that's what Marcus is always telling me.

She lies in bed, staring at her feet. Folding back the corner of the duvet, she lets out a deep sigh that she is sure must be loud enough to wake him. She moves closer and wriggles into him. Carefully, she rubs her cold hands against the back of his shins. He opens his mouth and licks the dryness of his lips. Amidst the fuzz of the alarm clock, she hears Ed Sheeran. She slams her fist down on the alarm button and lets out a long sigh, as quietly as she can. Slowly, he lifts his head from the pillow and looks at her.

Sheeran again? So, change the station?

I don't know how, she says.

His face darkens.

You refuse to listen to RTÉ, he says, where the music's better.

He remembers last week explaining to her that he didn't see the point in any other station. What he loved was the phone-ins, the stories of hardship, the women snatched by the nuns as babies, still living, still feeling pain, the men who just couldn't seem to stay out of prison no matter how hard they tried. Real life.

You smell terrible, he says, like a rank fox. Did you die in your sleep?

She ignores this. Georgia, she says, Shiv too, they're coming over soon, they'll be on their way over already.

Without saying anything, he snakes out of bed and heads into the bathroom. She listens to the tap run. A few seconds later – at least it feels like only seconds – the front door slams. Alone, she pads barefoot across the floorboards and into the living room where the cushions are crumpled from the night before. It had been a difficult night, waking, tossing and turning on the sofa, but she was growing used to it.

A medical journal lies open on the coffee table. Her fingers flick through until she lands on an image of an abdomen, gutted and raw. She swallows and turns the page. There is an illustration of a liver and a scalpel about to incise.

She hadn't been honest with June, certainly not about Tom. It had been an impulse decision to track him down on Twitter.

Yeah, I write now, paint, all kinds. Never been busier – you?

Had to think for a bit, but yeah of course I remember you! Got a woman now, a kid, a woman with a kid, not mine, but he's cute, calls me Dad. Not what I imagined – but you know how I was when we were kids, always a bit different. Truth is I never really seem to lead a normal…

The doorbell rings. Slowly, she rests her mug on top of the journal and glances at the oversized clock on the wall. She'd seen a similar one on a tube platform and paid a month's salary for it when they'd first moved in. Marcus hated it, called it pretentious, ticked too loudly.

The doorbell rings and she hauls herself up. On the damp step, Georgia stands with her arms outstretched, waiting for her a hug. Nancy's chin brushes against the woollen collar of Georgia's cardigan as she steps inside.

You smell nice, she says to Georgia.

Patchouli, light, not too strong, Georgia says. A Goth – but not too much.

Yes, come in, Nancy whispers, that's it. You don't need an invitation, do you?

Georgia returns to the door and peers down the street.

He's just around the corner trying to find a space, you know how he is. Round and round he goes, looking for the perfect slot, every time he does this. I would have found one much sooner.

Her small fingers clamp themselves around Nancy's thumb. Through her jersey dress, the bow of her iliac crest is a large, black heart. Her grey eyes are black in the amber light.

Earlier, before Marcus had woken, Nancy had looked at

herself in the bathroom mirror. It hadn't been the face she had expected to see, tiny red veins threading through her chin.

Judging by your face, Georgia says, dearest sister, it didn't go well, then?

In the living room, Georgia sits. Nancy watches her face jerk forward in fierce concentration, bird-like and curious. As Nancy readies herself to offer her a mug of coffee, the door rattles. Together they listen to the familiar squeak of trainers on the varnished wood. Nancy glances up to the light fittings, giant nipples, the brass tips hanging as if they are about to excrete milk. They listen to him throwing his shoes off in the hall. As he appears in the living room, a smile creeps up his face.

Nancy picks a knitting needle from the basket by her feet and grips it tight. She searches his face for signs of remorse or guilt or genuine regret. She doesn't have to look for long. Behind his glasses, he looks down, or sideways, she isn't sure.

Fists flying, Nancy says.

What did you say? Georgia asks, looking at her with wide eyes.

I said *fists flying*.

Nancy, you're not making any…

Shiv looks at them both. Nancy laughs. Shiv sits next to her on the arm of the chair. She dare not look at him. They are so close their sleeves are brushing, so close she can smell the washing powder on his jeans and the spiced musk of his skin. He pats her hand.

You've made enquiries about going back to work? Georgia asks her.

There's plenty of time for all that, he says, throwing Georgia a look. You'll go in your own time, won't you, Nancy?

Silence lingers in the air and it makes her feel as if she's shrinking. Her job at the bank was only meant to be a stop-gap, a change from teaching that had become too stressful for her. She wanted to work with money, a teller, someone who took money and recorded the transaction. Nothing more. But she had risen through the ranks quickly.

So you say, so you say, Nancy says. Funny how your words flow easily enough.

Georgia looks at Shiv and Shiv looks at Georgia.

Alone in her room, June looks around her. It would be nice to have new premises, the walls seem to press in and the)carpet has seen better days. She's tired, she realises, but her work for the day isn't complete. Slowly, she opens her laptop.

Partner A

N has one sibling, a younger sister. Her father is a deceased librarian and from her description it seemed as if he had very fixed ideas of how things should be. N felt that she respected her father but in the first consultation, as she spoke of him there was a sense that he may have been depressed and unable to manage situations that gave rise to strong, primitive feelings. She described turning to him following the marriage to her husband and writing to him with her concerns. N said his response was to minimise the situation and he told her that he planned to delete her email. N was clearly distressed by his response. Although she described her relationship with her mother as close, she also described her as 'cruel and insensitive'. It seemed as if she had become her mother's little partner and that this was the only way she was able to have some contact. Since the rupture in the relationship with her mother the younger sister seems to have moved into the role which was once N's. N described her mother as 'sitting, waiting to be needed'.

June closes the laptop. She'll head out soon and have a coffee somewhere before she heads home. Might do her good to move her feet, wake her up a bit, the stress of navigating the streets in rush hour will be reviving. Nancy Connell, one of the toughest cases she's come across yet. She had commented with a colleague in the staff room it was getting harder for her to make Nancy recognise her displacements and projections, of which there were many. There were worse cases, sure, but Nancy was so in love, it was hard to make her see just how much she could make happen for herself, if she could only allow herself to think differently about herself.

Nancy watches them through the hall window. Everything happens for a reason, Shiv had told her by email that grey day he'd moved in with Georgia and she'd wanted to believe him. She convinced herself she did believe him when she struggled with her suitcases up the drive the day she moved in with Marcus. She had every day of her life to look forward to, managed to convince herself all her troubles were over, nothing but beautiful days ahead of her.

He couldn't put his finger on what was hurting him so. But it was mighty. There might have been a time when he could shake himself out of the blues. When he was younger, in his twenties, he only looked forward. Not now. He wonders why that should be.

His parents' move from Ireland to London was a strange decision and one that could potentially have ruined his life. He had no reason to visit Dublin now. Not since Kim and him had lost touch.

The light reflecting on the white wall is a dull mustard hue and it helps to empty his mind. He suspects his mother, Shelagh, found him selfish. Earlier, lunch with her in Pret in the King's Road had been strained. She had remained mute on the matter of him and Nancy, but he could read her eyes, narrow and probing. It was an uncomfortable sensation, being judged by his mother. She didn't know the whole story. It was maddening.

The woman behind the counter, lacquered hair and a weak smile, hands him his list for the day. Sensing all eyes on him, once again he feels strangely small in the vastness of the ward. His eyes scroll down until they fix on a womb cancer case. Only once has he anaesthetised a woman under forty in such an operation. For him, this kind of thing was always sad.

She has lustrous dark hair and an elegant, feline pointed nose like Christy Turlington. She looks at him with small and frightened eyes and starts to cry. Through the gap in the curtain he watches her, little more than a lamb to the slaughter. She hugs her knees and he reminds himself he should be tougher and more business-like than this, and he wonders why, faced with her, he can't bring himself to be.

He drags a chair over from the next bed and takes a moment to breathe. He smiles his official smile and once again he is the robot who can pull himself through this. Lazily she looks past him to the patient in the next bed, a naked old woman, a soiled nightie scrunched in a ball at her feet. There is a strange smell. For a moment they watch the small of her back, heaving up and down as she sleeps.

If you like, he says, I can offer you a pre-med to help you relax.

I might die in there, she says. I want to be knocked out.

He looks down to his notes, not yet forty. On her arm, just below the hem of her t-shirt is a tattoo. The letter T is written in brown henna and he wonders who else is affected. Flesh forms a crescent under the bags of her eyes. Her hair is scraped back but a singular wisp trails down her back. It's so pretty he feels an urge to touch it.

Have you been in hospital before? Marcus asks.

He looks again at her name, but he somehow can't allow it to leave his lips.

Jessica, he says finally, have you been in hospital before?

She shakes her head. From across the space an explosion

of laughter disturbs the thin layer of silence in the ward. Fearfully, her eyes dart past his head to the nurses' station.

Does your family have a history of problems in operations? He asks.

Why? She asks, frightened. Is it dangerous in there for someone like me?

You'll be fine, really, it's just some problems can run in families.

He races down the page. When he does look up again, he sees her eyes are blank. He wants to stop writing and throw his pen across the ward. There is an urge to touch her arm, stronger than he has felt for a long while.

William's safety briefing begins in earnest, but Marcus isn't listening. He looks up, down and around, anywhere but at William. William hurries through his check-list and when he's finished, Marcus leads his team of students out of theatre to greet her. Lying flat, ready to be done, Jessica's face is soft and relaxed. Count to five, and by the time you reach five, you'll be under, he tells her, and then when all this is over you can go back to your glorious life, okay? Rising in his throat is burning acid, a wave of nausea. He breathes in deeply. The heated air in the basement is fetid, metallic and it makes him feel heavy.

Marcus starts her with a generous dose of fentanyl. He connects the propofol and starts the TCI pump. As she's falling under, he sluices her through with a muscle relaxant. Go into the sweet night now, beautiful one, he thinks. It's safe in there, trust me. He ventilates her. Asabi puts on the flowtrons and helps him intubate. Carefully, he tapes her eyes and pushes the temperature probe deep into her oesophagus, feeling her soul puncture. Slowly, he disconnects the monitors and the breathing circuit. When he's done he closes his eyes and breathes. Asabi, he senses, is still beside him. He opens his eyes. After he's overseen her transfer from the bed to the operating table, he watches the theatre team position her. Slowly, he adjusts her warming blanket. When he's done, he clicks his pen and begins writing. William washes his hands and buffs them with a paper towel. The wiry Romanian nurse wipes the patient's abdomen with antiseptic, ready for the knife. Marcus moves between trying to complete his notes and making sure the anaesthetic balance is exactly right. As William slices, Marcus holds his breath. Deftly, William pulls out her womb and Marcus retreats into the anaesthetics room.

Hovering by his laptop still open at his desk, he looks at the room he knows as well as his own study: the black swivel chair, walls the colour of grey hairs that now pepper his hair. He turns on his laptop and glances at the opening chapter of his report. The words jump up and zap his smarting eyes. As he tries to focus on his opener, he's disturbed by laughter in theatre. It fades and in its place is the sound of steel chiming against steel. The steady electrical breathing of the monitor relaxes him a little until the laughter starts up again. It is Asabi. Delivering that one spectacularly badly, he thinks.

She can never reach the punchline without her confidence faltering.

He closes his eyes. Behind him, there's a dripping sound, constant, unidentified. He zones out, hoping nobody will ask him any questions, stupid questions that are incongruous when he is upset and stumbling around for meaning. And bloody hell, if it could have been anyone other than William.

An hour after leaving the house, after a few false turns down arterial corridors that lead to nowhere, she finds herself alone outside his consultancy room. The door to his office is blue, blue to match her mood.

Hoping to see signs of life in his department, to share the exotic happenings in a busy, London hospital, taste the drama beyond closed doors, she waits, unsure what to do next. The hospital is as quiet as her house in Fulham. This is not what she expected.

Cautiously, she knocks. Chris opens the door and her painted-on smile drops. Standing with his legs just a few inches too wide, Chris reaches out to shake her hand. She remembers, of course, Marcus would be teaching on a Monday.

Good to see you, Nancy, he says. Can I, shall I take this?

Without waiting for a response, he takes Marcus's lunch box from her hand. Suddenly, she's aware how strange it is for her to be here like this, the pathetic little woman bringing him a sandwich. She feels smaller than the steel flask of coffee in her bag.

I'll take that too, that's it, come on in, *all* the way in. Won't you sit down? He's away but you can wait here if you like. Fine with me if you do.

He sits at his desk and swivels his chair to face her, grinning for a beat too long.

Awkward? She asks.

What's that you're saying?

Me being here like this?

What?

I was just saying, an awkward day to catch him. I forgot it was Monday.

You forgot it was Monday last week too, Nancy, but no matter.

Did I?

She follows the line of his gaze. He flashes his eyes back to his laptop, hits the space bar and grins at something or other he's reading. She thinks his teeth are appalling, like the charred panels of a burnt, wooden pier.

Stay as long as you like, Nancy. That is, that's if you don't mind me working away here like this?

She wants to laugh.

No, I think I'll just leave this on his desk, if I may, if I can just – won't keep you. Need to get going, really.

Fractiously, she pulls at her ponytail. There isn't a doctor in the land that can put her at ease. She is jealous of their status and usefulness. Forcing another smile now, she hopes Chris will be too busy to notice the crack in her smile. She wants him to say something, anything. She recalls Marcus had told her about Chris's wife, The Sense of Entitlement Nurse, or SEN as Marcus had labelled her, after she'd left Chris for a private surgeon. Marcus had suspected that had been her plan all along.

Oh sure, he says without looking away from his email.

There is a long spell of silence until at last he rises out of his seat, makes for the door and pulls it open.

But listen, he says, good to see you, Nancy.

He places his hand on her elbow, close enough for her to smell his warm breath, a stale bag of cheese and onion crisps. The skin on his lips is dry and chapped.

Marcus told me – I hope you don't – but I've been taking an interest, he says. Anyway, at least now you've had a rest you can think about going back to work, because it might be time now? Sometimes these things are out of our control and besides, there are lots of people in your situation.

Yes, Chris. So right, Chris, she wants to say. Thanks for reminding me. So clever of you, because I hadn't actually processed any of this for myself.

Well, so long, then, he says. I'll be sure to pass on your lunch to Marcus.

When the door is closed behind her, she heads down the corridor. With no idea if she'll be able to find the right department, she keeps walking. Wandering past an abandoned trolley, busy nurses brush past her. She follows the light until it bends and brightens. She arrives at the entrance to a waiting room. Oncology.

She pulls her tortoiseshell Wayfarers from her bag. Slowly,

she peers through the lenses. There are bored, exhausted faces everywhere, some with hair, some without. All around her are milk-white dolls in synthetic wigs. A blonde woman with short hair reads, another picks fluff from her mohair jumper. On electric scales, a patient waits. The nurse reads the digital display to her and scribes something in her pad. Nancy's eyes stop roaming. There's one face, familiar. She stands motionless, staring at his auburn hair. She considers turning back and returning to Marcus's department. She looks again. It's a risky strategy meeting him here, but she reasons the hospital was a big place.

He slides his arm around his partner and Nancy feels a pang. She immediately recognises it as a wave of envy. Nervously, she rests her palms on the reception desk and steadies herself. Ready for her query, the receptionist looks up from her Sudoku and widens the tips of her mouth in an official smile. Nancy braves a glance back at the man she'd brought back to life in her recent session with June. His hair is shaved close to his scalp now. Most of all, she wants to study Tom's wife, the woman he's chosen, the woman who is staring dead-eyed into the middle distance.

So now we've been chatting for a few days, I'll fess up, can't really keep it a secret, it's taking up too much of my time. She's being treated at Barts. My wife. Not much time to go into it all now, but I'll tell you more later. Not sure she'll make it yet. Sorry if my contact might be a bit intermittent in the meantime, can't help that at the moment. It's her kid I'm most worried for. Well, I would be, wouldn't I? And in answer to your question I was trying to remember – when was it 1990? 1991? We were in that tiny box room of mine. The Sundays were playing on the tape player. You liked The Sundays. People I know, places I go, make me feel tongue-tied. I can't believe I've remembered those lyrics after all these years. They've been stuck somewhere in my head all this time (and no, I didn't google them). So being as I win, what's my prize?

The receptionist coughs, bringing her back but Nancy keeps her eyes fixed on him. She studies his eyelashes in the light. They're shorter and fairer than Marcus's. Suddenly, the receptionist stops smiling and the waiting area begins to move with life again. A patient's name is called and a woman in a paisley head scarf hauls her thin frame across the room. The consultant greets her under the arch and shakes her hand. Tom waits with his eyes closed, resting his chin on his wife's head. Her hair, she thinks, is the colour of camomile tea. Others around them stare blankly into smart phones.

Praying Tom won't open his eyes before the doors open, she makes for the lift. The doors open. She risks a final glance back. This time he looks at her, forcing her to swallow. He strokes his wife's hair with long, gentle fingers.

Marcus stares at the watch on his wrist. The seconds close in to midnight. Time means less and less to him these days.

This morning, as it was growing light outside, she'd thrown his mobile at him smashing it into tiny pieces. Shards of plastic had scattered everywhere and landed in the plant pot, under the television, in the fibres of the rug. In unison they'd both surveyed the damage. He'd grabbed his uniform, still creased from the arm of the chair and made out the door. Exiting from the tube at Chancery Lane, he'd pounded the pavement, his mind numbed against her and the rest of the world.

As he pulls out his spare mobile from his pocket, he sees there is a text from Nancy. She's still upset, she tells him, but she doubts he even cares.

He is changed into his work clothes and he kicks open the door to theatre. To his relief, William is nowhere to be seen, golfing in St Andrew's for the weekend.

A quick glance at the rota informs Marcus who's on instead, a semi-retired neurosurgeon he's worked with before, Harry Gornell. Harry was retired but occasionally covered the odd graveyard shift. He'd long had him penned as a decent man, a little stiff but a good worker.

Harry emerges from the drugs room and nods at Marcus. Marcus watches him move around the patient, a girl of fourteen with smooth skin. The day person has already put the breathing tube in.

So young, much too young for this, Harry says, a complication needing an emergency drainage on her brain. Still, shouldn't take more than a couple of hours, if all goes to plan.

Marcus nods. His head hurts behind his eyes. Inflating oneself can be a mistake, his father Frank had warned him once, probably at the same breakfast table his mother had imparted unwanted advice, it's a mistake because there's a long way to fall. He wonders why he's only remembering this now.

Standing well back from the slab, he watches Harry fumble, his forehead glossy, struggling to slide the drain in. Marcus recalls even William had problems with this side of preparation. Harry checks the clock behind Marcus's head. Marcus waits.

Damn it all, Harry says. I'll have to call a more experienced consultant in from home. BRB.

Struggling to keep his eyes open and alert, Marcus eyes the theatre team hovering around him. The silence in the room makes him feel dizzy, but he has no idea why. There is another round of hand-washing. The scrub nurse sits, crosses her legs and resumes her Sudoku. Lana, the wiry Romanian whispers something in the ear of the junior anaesthetist. Marcus half-listens to her tale of leopard-skin handcuffs and a snapped key.

He leaves them to it and disappears into the side room. He could read another one of Chris's joke circulars. He could send another text to Nancy. Five-or-so minutes pass, ten, twenty. He decides he will send a text to Nancy. He will tell her he understands only too well about her moods. Slowly, he moves his thumb over his mobile. He remembers an earlier text he'd sent to her where he'd said it was fine for her to lash out, or something empathetic like that. Asabi glides past him, fuzzy, just in shot. He is about to text Nancy when his phone buzzes with a message.

Talking to yourself again, Marcus, Asabi says, want to watch that.

He looks at Asabi. She smiles. He doesn't return her smile. This time his phones buzzes with another text, from Nancy.

Why are you being like this? I'm sorry about your phone. I'll get you a new one. If that's all you've got to worry about, you're lucky, aren't you?

Infuriated, he hammers out a reply. When he's finished, he looks at Asabi, her full lips smeared with gloss, watching him. At the weekends, where the nurses were once framed nicely in his thoughts – sexy uniforms, helpful smiles – he often thought of Asabi. At least, he had from time to time.

Playfully, Asabi takes his phone from his hand, hauls him up out of his chair and pushes him towards the door back to theatre. When he is back in theatre he sees Harry is still away trying to find help. The others are busy talking among themselves, so he does what he needs to: he checks on the girl and her equipment. She's stable, he decides. Her oxygen saturations are lower than he would like: 92-3% compared to 96+, but not an immediate concern. After adjusting the settings on the alarms to take account of this, fixing them so they won't go off every five minutes, he returns to his room.

Asabi slumps next to him. Over coffee with Chris he had tried to talk to him about the presumptuous way she has, but at the last moment he'd changed his mind, easier to spirit her away. Her hair is straightened and scraped back. It's severe, but he thinks it suits her, makes her look older, more his age.

Following her gaze to the clock on the wall, he sees an hour has passed since Harry left theatre.

Kicking back his chair, he stares up at the ceiling and breathes out long and slow. Asabi returns to her laptop beside him. It had been Asabi's passion for the job of anaesthetics which attracted him at first. When they met, he was aware Asabi was eager to please him, in awe even.

My wife, he says, will be in limbo waiting for me, beside herself with boredom, knitting another square – knitting? She must miss the glamour of another bank transaction, surely?

Maybe, Asabi says.

Intuitively, he knew she had compromised a piece of herself in being his wife, and this irritated him without fully understanding why. He'd loved sex with her but he'd thought about new body shapes too: the curve of other hips and the newness of fresh skin. His wavering indifference – and it did waver – boiled down to one simple fact: He'd wanted to live his life.

He decides he'll call Nancy and tell her he's sorry. He'll tell her tomorrow night is his night off and he'll treat her, take her somewhere nice. After he's pressed her name on his keypad, he waits for her to pick up. As she croaks a hello, he slams the phone down on his desk and heads back into theatre. Still no Harry. Sensing the others' eyes on him, he takes a look at the monitor. His strained smile signals to the others she's fine, but to ensure he's not interrupted again he switches off the alarm and heads back to his room.

He picks up the phone and calls again. She answers immediately, but this time she sounds a little brighter. She tells him she's been on the exercise bike in the spare room. After he's hung up he stretches his arms up to the ceiling.

Asabi taps his shoulder, her signal it is time for her break. Focused again, he goes back in to check on the girl. The others watch him study the monitor. A minute-or-so passes. Swallowing, he watches the theatre door swing open.

Harry returns with another consultant. The man's shirt is unbuttoned and his bow tie is loosened. Marcus imagines he must be unhappy to be called in from home on a Saturday night, anyone would be. Staring disbelieving at the slab, Harry locks eyes with Marcus. The walls appear to quiver like a palpitating heart muscle. All is silent.

Nancy places a black and grey mug, his favourite, under the Espresso machine. She presses the button, once, twice, three times. Under the gargling whir, she can hear the sound of all too familiar sighs in the next room. There is a dark thud of his trainers as they smash against the wall. Then, silence.

She finds him sat forward on the sofa, rubbing the stubble on his chin. She hands him his coffee, her second attempt to make it the way he likes it. As if trying to warm the atmosphere in the living room, the morning light shines through the window, exposing a thin patch of hair on the back of his head.

The girl, he says. It all happened so fast, just a blur. She was breathing and then she wasn't. Not like me to – I don't make mistakes, you know that.

She sits next to him and wraps her fingers around his thumb. He pushes her hand away.

Christ, what a fucking disaster, he says.

You're not a…

Fourteen. That's how old she was. Bloody rare enough for a girl that age to have that type of cancer. There was a prob – a big one. A problem positioning her tube. No, before you ask, of course I didn't do the right kind of checks. My head was spinning with it all, our argument, I mean. She had a heart attack. Died. She died. How the fuck could I have been so slack?

He slumps back and stares up at the ceiling. The look on his face scares her.

That's very sad to hear, she says. But how is it your fault?

He tightens his fists so hard she hears his joints crack.

How is it my fault? Sad? It's worse than that. I didn't do the right type of checks, that's how it's my fault. She was in for an abscess drainage, had pneumonia, her oxygen levels were falling and I didn't pick it up. Didn't give her the care she deserved. She put her life in my hands and I let her down. Stupid. Dangerous. Cunt. Don't do that, you're after giving me that sad, disappointed look. It wasn't just me, there was a series of errors. A combination of the pneumonia and the wrongly positioned tube made her dangerously hypoxic. The tube was too far down, only one lung ventilated.

Suddenly, he stops and throws her a look.

Why am I wasting my breath? He asks her. I should have taken more care.

Did you put the tube in? She asks.

Did I? No.

Nancy's head spins with the information that's been flying at her, only a fraction of which she fully understands. Once again she realises how little she knows about what exactly it is he does in there.

Look, it's like this, he says. In the changeover important checks were missed. I should have made sure it was okay, that's my responsibility. I can't pin that on anyone else. But I was tired. I tried *so* hard to concentrate.

She tunes in to the sounds on the street outside, an engine running and a car door slamming. She can hear his breathing, light, regular, controlled. He tells her there'll be an investigation, of course there will be. He looks at her, and it scrapes her so much she could be naked wading through bramble. He has forms to fill in, he tells her, and he'll be making a start tonight.

I had to sign my name at the bottom, he says. Imagine putting your name to that! But the others – they just went home as usual, saw them walk silently to their cars. It was desperate. They just didn't know what to say to me. Now they really do – they really do hate me.

They must have wondered how they could have prevented it too? They must be feeling like they failed every bit as much as you?

She swallows to see a dark look transform his face. In

matters requiring tact, she knows she's incapable of saying the right thing, at least with him. Slowly, she turns to face the open window. Pellets of hail clamber their way in; tiny iron crow bars. She leaps up to close the window. Staring at the television, she sees elephants walking in line through the Saharan sands.

Look how their ears swing, she says.

What?

Without warning, he grabs her cheek and turns her face to face his. He smiles, but when she cautiously smiles back his mouth hardens again.

Cold now, she wraps her cardigan tight around her body. She sees the shadows along the top of his cheeks and under his eyes.

You're frightening me, she says, it's your moods, they're designed to keep me away.

Ignoring her, he stands and moves towards the door.

I suppose you're going to follow me, he says.

But he doesn't wait for a response.

Frozen to the sofa, she pulls the orange blanket up to her neck. She listens to him slam the bedroom door shut.

Marcus lies back, staring at the closed door, trying to stitch together all the happenings of his terrible night. What he wants is to be left alone, perhaps forever. It exhausts him explaining what goes on at the hospital. His phone buzzes in his pocket. Asabi.

Whenever you feel like you want to talk, you know I'm here for you. You never doubted that, did you? xx

Asabi presses the steaming iron to the cuffs of her shirt. She presses hard and wonders how long she will have to press before the cotton singes. Her mind races with possibilities. If she leaves the house now with the iron resting on the cuff, it won't take long for the shirt to catch fire and the whole house to burn down. Right now, she is sure she couldn't give a damn. What she is sure of is she would like to further examine this feeling. There is Marcus, and his mysterious wife at home and there is a pain in her heart.

Walsh lies back in bed and glances over Marcus's notes. He turns to face his husband and smiles. Darling, he says, it's clear to me I have all the evidence I need. Judging by the quality of this paper alone, this doctor isn't fit for office.

Gently, she opens the door of the bedroom. With his knees clutched to his chest, he stuffs his phone back in his pocket and gestures her in with a flick of his head. She perches uneasily on the edge of the bed.

The thing is, he says, when other people make mistakes, it bothers me more than anything. It bothers me more than death, and it's always there, the chance they might. I'm the brightest, the best, they all know this. I'm the one they come running to in an emergency – and there's always one problem or other. Asabi went for her break. Check. Did I say she could? No? Yes? Think, man, think. Did she actually ask me if she could? Ah, what difference does it make? It won't make any difference, I can't lay this on her. With or without her, I should have done my job properly – and why didn't I?

He looks down to her bare feet. He sees her coral polish is chipped. Another thing she's forgotten to fix.

I'm the best at what I do, he says. This is the one certainty in all this. Now I've lost the trust it's taken twenty years of working my bollocks off to achieve. So now it's my fault, I don't know what to do. Twenty years of never putting a foot wrong. Christ, what have I done to deserve this?

Do you want me to go away, Marcus?

What? Maybe.

Does it irritate you me being here?

He doesn't answer. She twists her body round, and with fear fighting common sense inside her, pulls him to her. As she listens to him breathe she tries to forget how cold it was between them last time. Whatever happens, she doesn't want it to be like the last time.

The bathroom mirror is smeared with toothpaste. She rubs it with the hem of her t-shirt. On her grey t-shirt the word 'dreamer' is printed in rainbow colours. That'll be right, Marcus had said to her recently, more and more like that infantile t-shirt every day. Her phone buzzes in her pocket, but she's not in the mood for weakness, she's in the mood for strength. She leaves the bathroom and slips back into the darkness of the living room. All is quiet in the street outside. She feels stupid to be crying when he's the one who's suffering. She has to stay calm. Her phone buzzes in her pocket. As she looks at the screen she sees it's 3am. It's Tom.

Can't say for sure. It's sad to see her suffering like this, but it's amazing what they can do now. Anyway, good of you to come and meet me, I really needed to see you. You looked different too, I wouldn't have known you if you hadn't been staring at me like that in the waiting room. Life's hard, isn't it? I guess… I guess we didn't know that back then. Anyway, yes to meeting up again. Somewhere quieter next time?

She tries to remember the letter he'd sent from Oxford all those years ago. He missed her, he said, but if he had a cup of tea, he could manage. It was lonely when he thought about home, his friends and her. She wonders if that could have been true, that he'd missed her.

The first he knew of it was a text from Nancy. He wonders if there would ever be an end to his obligations.

You're not going to be too late, are you? It's just Anna's gone to all this effort and Georgia's coming. You remember?! I told you Georgia called this morning to remind us. You can't have forgotten?

On the half-empty tube, he reads her text message over and over. Georgia, he's said to Nancy recently, a noxious little bitch, poison ivy. Always playing games. A text pings on his phone. He knows before looking it will be her.

It's me again. Whenever you get the chance and Nancy's not around, get in touch. I'm sorry I took a break when I did. I'm sorry I wasn't there for you when this terrible thing happened.

She's a coward, he thinks, only able to show warmth by text. He intimidates her and the thought of this never failed to excite him.

Earlier, she'd been due in work and he dreaded having to face her, but he needn't have worried, she'd called in sick. When he'd left theatre, William had given him no doubt he'd heard what had happened. His smile had been strange, not the usual one-upmanship, the smile designed to make him feel insignificant, but it had been a look of concern.

Emerging from Mile End tube, the damp air blasts his face. He walks past a shopkeeper putting out trays of blood oranges. The shopkeeper pulls at his sleeve and asks him how he is. Strange, he mutters to the man, what's London coming to?

Earlier, his headache had been so intense he'd toyed again with the idea of raiding the drugs cabinet, until he remembered about the two grubby Ibuprofens gathering dust in the bottom of his bag. He'd picked them out of his rucksack and swallowed them instead. He looks down to his hands.

He arrives at Anna's yellow door and knocks. Behind him on the trunk road he hears the sound of a throat collating spit. It sounds like a strangled kind of gargle and he turns around to see who the culprit could be, but it's too syrupy-dark to see. From beyond the door, he hears a voice, laughter and the sound of a door being slammed.

Anna answers. With a weak smile, she opens the door. Leonora peers at him from the top of the stairs through narrow, wooden slats. She wears a pyjama top with a unicorn emblazoned on the front, ice-cream stained.

Embarrassed to be empty-handed more than he is to be over an hour late, he steps inside. Before he has a chance to deliver an apology, Shiv appears as if from nowhere and Marcus's headache worsens. Shiv's hair, slicked high with gel looks more phallic than natural. A single chest hair creeps above the top of his linen blue shirt. He hands Marcus a shot glass filled with purple liquid.

It's rich, Shiv says. Too thick for me but try it. Tastes good enough for you? We bought it in Porto last week. Fascinating place, have you been?

Marcus takes off his jacket. Anna takes it from him and carefully drapes it over a chair. He takes the glass from Shiv's hand and gulps the port down. Guarded, he hands the empty glass to Shiv.

No comment, Marcus says.

Shiv and Anna head into the open plan kitchen and Marcus follows. Reluctantly he nods to the others around the table. He thinks the kitchen looks bigger, more expensive than he remembers, marbled, smooth. He wonders how much her husband left her in his will.

Beyond the glass of the French doors are bottles of lager lined up by the stone wall. As he ponders opening the doors and grabbing one, Nancy rises from her seat and softly kisses him on his cheek.

Sorry everyone, she says, don't mind my husband. He's been too busy saving lives to give us a second thought.

A little waspish, he hisses.

Come on, not like you, Nancy says, a little too loudly.

Knowing how the land lies, how he can do so without anyone minding, he slides open the door and helps himself to a bottle.

Portuguese, will have to do, he says.

He wonders why his wife is looking at him that way.

Sorry everyone, he says, the thing is I find it hard to switch off after work. First law of physics is the energy waves are always carried over. This can't be helped of course but still, there it is, I'm here now.

He pulls out a chair next to Nancy, snakes his arm around her and feels her shoulders stiffen. Nancy's head whirs with all the booze flushing through her system. He's here, she can relax but despite herself, she wants to single-handedly plough through the remainder of the wine bottle resting on the table.

Shiv moves his chair closer to Marcus. Marcus grins at Shiv, but she knows this grin, the grin that says: *hey I know you've fucked my wife, but no hard feelings, eh?* She studies them together. On the surface, Marcus is polite, nodding in all the right places, but she sees the knuckles of his hand are as white as his dinner plate. Her thoughts rewind to Tom in the hospital coffee shop, sobbing as she'd held him.

Georgia sits upright in her chair and pats Anna's hand.

So, you remembered I'm vegan now, Georgia says to Anna, but I'll leave the aubergine if you don't mind. And the mushrooms. No, no need to apologise, you weren't to know I despise mushrooms.

Anna smiles, but Nancy notices, only just.

Marcus pushes his chicken in Riesling around his plate. Nancy wonders if Tom is vegetarian too. She wonders if he even liked the coffee she'd bought him, he hadn't touched it in the ground floor café at Bart's. Nancy senses a shift in the room. Leonora appears at the door, her eyes red as if she's been crying. She slides over to Nancy and rests her hand on her leg.

I did well today, Leonora says.

You sound a little sulky, Nancy says, as if someone has pierced you with a pin and let all your air out.

Full marks for my algebra test, Leonora says. Mr Harper, that's my teacher, tall with a very long moustache, he moved me up a set.

So, why the long face?

Leonora shrugs. Gently, Anna places her fork down, leans back and smiles.

Any opportunity to tell us how clever she is, Anna says. They say competition's not healthy but Leo's proof kids love tests.

But Nancy's mind floats in and out her time with Tom. Anna had told her once her feelings always showed on her face, and this had scared Nancy, better to be alone at a time like this. Georgia clears her throat.

Did I tell you about Pisa? Georgia asks. It was so funny there, not at all what we were expecting. The leaning tower was like a punched wedding cake. Well, that's what Shiv said, didn't you, darling? No, don't bother, Pisa's a dead town.

Still, we caught the train from there to Florence, only about eight euros for the entire trip. Italy, crazy prices compared to here. So poor but their trains – Shiv will tell you, won't you? There was snow and frost all through the Tuscan hills. It really was like a Winterbottom film, wonderful.

Nancy flits her eyes over Georgia's head. Chocolate sauce bubbles in a copper pan, and she wonders what else Anna can afford on a teacher's salary. She knows her boyfriend Sebastian's no help.

Anna's first husband, Tim, had died in the shower. It had been the week before his thirtieth birthday. Anna had been helping out with the school netball team, which was typical of her to go beyond the minimum expected of her as a teacher. It was the B team regional finals, and she'd come home only to find him slumped on the floor. The towel he'd used to dry himself lay abandoned, soaked through on the floor beside him as he lay in the foetal position. She noticed Anna spoke about him less these days. These days it was all about Sebastian.

Nancy glances across the table. She watches Marcus asking Shiv various questions of little importance. *How are your shares doing? Have you made a killing lately?* Shiv, as he had done in the past, mistakes Marcus's passive aggression for a genuine connection and leans in closer to him. Suddenly, she is afraid for Shiv. Like a trucker, Marcus wipes his mouth with the back of his hand. Clumsily, he shunts his chair in closer to Shiv. Shiv grins.

Leonora lifts her hand from Nancy's leg, kisses her on the

cheek, and kisses the others goodnight. When Leonora has left them all, Nancy breathes out her relief. Anna grabs her hand.

You know you're her favourite, Anna says. She's been asking all week what day you're coming. She's been practising that song, you know the one? Voice of an angel but, well, you know Leo, no confidence. She really does need to get past that if she wants to be famous like she says.

Anna gathers up the dinner plates. Nancy pulls her back down.

Look at Shiv, Nancy whispers. He really thinks Marcus is interested in what he has to say. Too bad his parents made him feel so small about himself.

What do you mean, Shiv's doing well for himself?

I know, but he's an estate agent, not a doctor.

So?

Well, we know that's good, but his bloody parents don't think so. Anyway, look at him kissing Marcus's arse – pathetic. Why would he lower himself like that? Marcus doesn't care about him.

Anna smiles.

I know, Anna says.

Leonora, is she okay? She was quieter than usual?

I keep trying to coach her to be a bit braver, Anna says, but it's hard-going. You know, she actually thinks you're going to take her to auditions in London one day? She actually thinks you're going to be her agent.

Nancy grips her wine glass tight.

Georgia's unusually quiet, Nancy whispers, a high priestess keeping it all inside, not sharing what she really thinks.

Georgia, appearing not to hear nonetheless looks at them both.

It's great you have such a bond with Leo, Georgia says. It's nicer maybe with friends' kids, because sometimes being related can muddy the waters. You can be too emotional when it's all in the family, can't you?

On the other side of the table, Marcus has heard enough. He has to get away from Shiv, from his world of property and money, where people don't matter, never have. He glances at Nancy and wonders why she's staring at him. For a second Nancy and Marcus lock eyes. Finally, feeling light again, he pulls at his shirt and stands.

Shiv knows, Marcus says, don't you Shiv?

Knows what? Shiv asks, startled.

All about virility, Marcus says.

Marcus, this isn't the time or…

What do you mean? Why not? Go on, what are you waiting for? Tell them! You know today I received a text from Shiv, Marcus says, asking if he could tell me something important. And I told him, sure go right ahead. Ha, you're bristling now, aren't you? I can see little beads of sweat on your forehead. Come on now, what is it? What is it you want to tell us? We're all waiting.

Tired of waiting for him to speak, Marcus grabs his arm. Slowly Nancy puts down her wine glass.

What the fuck is going on, Marcus? She asks, aware her voice sounds shaky. I'm drunk, but not drunk enough for…

Come on, Marcus goads. You might as well, Shiv. We're going to find out sooner or later.

Shiv slumps with his head in his hands and it is then she registers the gear shift in the room. All the violent, jumbled words of the past minutes explode in her head and she silently pleads for her husband to consider her feelings for once. She stays perfectly still and wonders if they can all see through her automatic smile – a dead-eyed smile from a woman who has since stopped breathing. Finally, she stands and as she does so her fork clangs to the floor. In her panicked scramble, she kicks it to Georgia with her foot. Georgia sits back and rubs her stomach, girlish and proud. Anna who has been quiet, rubs mascara from under her eye and sighs.

It's true, Georgia says. I'm sorry to say but look, I know but well it's not the kind of thing we can – we can't keep it a secret forever.

Georgia looks at her, then to Marcus and back to her again. Nancy grabs her empty glass, wishing it was full again.

Across the table, Marcus sits down and relaxes back. Next to him, slumped forward with his head in his hands, Shiv emits an audible simper. Whether this is with relief or with sorrow, she has no way of knowing.

With whisky still warming his brain, he only half listens to her. As they snake between Earls Court and Fulham Broadway on the District line, he resigns himself to a stalemate. He knows she's vying for a reaction – any reaction. Her accusations so far have been sniping bullets and she keeps them coming.

Christ, look at that snogging couple, he says, passion, intoxication, boredom? They look deranged. Must be a full moon. He's definitely more into it than her. Devouring, tongues, wet mouths and…

What?

Those two over there, he says.

Please Marcus, listen to me.

Why should…?

Don't pretend you – being all pally with Shiv like that, like you were – you don't normally give him the time of day. And why were you late? *So* late. I needed you there. I needed your – your *support*. You sat at the other end of the table. I kissed you – and…

She looks down to her hands.

You're like a little girl, he hisses, pulling at the bobbles on your mittens.

Fuck off, she says. It was – everyone must wonder – you couldn't have been on time, not even tonight. God knows I'm not always in the mood myself. All that falseness.

Exactly, he says. Small talk is a waste of my time.

They arrive at their stop. He stands, willing the doors to open. When they do he jumps out and purposefully doesn't look back to check if she's following. He knows she will be. He can recognise her sulking footsteps anywhere.

As he runs up the steps he resists the urge to scream.

He pushes through the open barrier. After a moment of hesitation, he heads in the direction of the cemetery. As he nears the locked gates, he turns around to see if she's caught up. There is no sign of her and he wants to keep moving. Slowly, he trudges the long way home along the trunk road.

Back at the house, he stands at the small window in the hall. A few minutes pass in silence, one, two, three, four.

With her eyes wild and drunken, she falls up the steps and swipes the door with her keys. He backs away towards the coat stand and watches as she shoots past him, leaving him to guess which room she's disappeared in to. There is a squeak of leather in the living room. He heads into the kitchen and pours himself a whisky. After a minute or two passes, she comes in and joins him there. Standing with her back to the fridge, her purple pumps shine under the ceiling lights.

Look, he says, even your nostrils are flaring. You can't resist divilment, can you? Can't back down. Beyond you.

It was obvious, she says. Why did you rise to his bait? You made him say it. *You* were the one who – *you* not Shiv. Because he didn't want to spoil the party. You goaded him. You made him…

Marcus grabs her arm. She tries to struggle free.

Yeah, that's how it was, he says. I mean at least I can see how it must have looked. But there's no reasoning with you. You can't reason with someone determined to play the victim. Drunken idiot.

Who, me? She asks.

You need to be tucked away from the world, he says.

Where no-one can find you, self-pitying bitch that you are tonight. Forget Shiv. You know how he can be. I – I just couldn't take it. Not after the day I – look, he was bursting at the seams. What a virile specimen. And guess what he did, he only goes and tells me about it by text. By *text*. He was itching – itching for us to find out. To remind you what you're missing. But you're stuck with me now, aren't you? Look at me, look at me when I'm talking to you. Straight in the eyes, that's it. Christ, I couldn't bear to be at that tedious dinner a second longer.

Why did you do it? She asks.

Do what? Why does it even matter?

Slowly, she rubs his cheek.

Couldn't you – couldn't you have got me on my own first?

Look, I didn't – he – Shiv.

Nancy moves closer to him. She is close enough for him to be able to kiss her. She starts to cry. He fights down an impulse to grab and shake her. He wants to tell her the truth, that Shiv had begged him by text not to say anything, not to mention it before he had a chance to speak with her himself.

One nil to Georgia your *sister*. The selfish one.

He feels a hand on his.

Because she wanted to hurt you, he says. She doesn't care about you. The problem is – always has been – you give her too much, too much of yourself and she doesn't deserve it. She's a schemer, that's the truth, likes to win.

Nancy pulls her hand away.

Who the hell are you to talk about competitiveness? No, Marcus, that's your game. Sometimes I think that's all you are.

Well, I have to be. It's the only way I can pay for this place.

He turns his back on her and peers out of the window. The shed, his sanctuary, invites him. More than anything he wants to head out there and hide. Fractiously, his eyes dart towards the dish above the cooker for the key, but he sees the dish is empty. He brushes past her. With no other option, he throws open the door to the living room. Crashing down on the sofa so heavily he knocks her knitting from the arm, his mind whirs. She appears by the door.

I don't understand you, she whispers.

Don't you? Well, then, let me tell you about your sister...

He watches her pull at her hair.

How can you call someone so fragile a monster? She asks. Christ!

She looks at him and he looks away.

The shed, he says, I could scream in there, a loud, primal howl. Did it when I was a kid to find out how far my lungs would stretch. Jesus, my head is splitting with the stress of it all. You're smiling – why?

She grabs her blanket and slumps down in the armchair, facing him.

Look, he says, you can believe what you want about your sister. That's something I can't control. I can't *make* you see. But I'll tell you this again: She likes to win.

Nancy squirms with it all, the dissonance in her head, the need to be close to him and the need to fight for her sister. As a wife, a daughter, a sister, she wonders if she's ever been given the opportunity to be herself. Who would she be without any of these labels? It would be an adventure to find out.

Well, maybe it's true, she says. I sometimes wonder about Georgia too. Oh, I don't know. It's late – too late for all this. Need bed.

She's rises from her seat and heads to the door, but as she risks a glance back at him, he is slumped with his head in his hands. It makes her pause for a second. Was this silence him inviting her over?

Look at the evidence, he says. She took Shiv from you, didn't she?

She stiffens, puts one foot in front of the other and makes for the door, then stops again.

I let Shiv go to her, she says slowly, deliberately, because I wanted to, I wanted *you*.

He lifts his head. She sees now his eyes are red.

She didn't waste any time though, did she? After wielding her bony little claws in like that.

I'm asking you nicely now, Nancy says. Don't speak about her like that. You think I haven't already processed this in my head already?

She doesn't care, that's all, he says sharply. It's all an act. That sickly way she has of pretending she's only trying to help you.

For a moment, they're silent again. She glances at the oversized clock on the wall. The time is already past midnight. She removes her glasses and stares past him to the candle.

Did I leave that burning? She asks. Was I in such a rush to get to the party? I can't even trust myself.

She stares at the flickering flame until it becomes a stemless dandelion head, floating and flashing. The hospital, Tom, the woman with camomile hair, his wife, it all rises flame-like in her head.

He gets up and brushes past her but she follows him into the bedroom. When he pushes her onto the bed, she lets him battle his way inside her. She tries to draw him nearer but he might as well be fucking the coat stand in the hall.

The leaves fall on the damp ground, burnt umber and golden. Kicking them in her cerise boots, Leonora continues her tirade of whining, a proliferation of *But Why's*.

But it's Saturday, and you *said* I'm allowed sweets on a Saturday.

Across from them in the café by the pond, pigeons swarm on leftovers. To the right of the pigeons, a couple walk silently with a greyhound. Anna puts her hands in her pockets and rustles some sweet papers. When she's bored with kicking the leaves, Leonora sandwiches herself between them on the bench.

It was an unexpected blow, Nancy says. Of course it was.

The faint sound of rustling sweet papers stops. A bird swoops low and there is crunch of gravel. Pedalos roped up by the edge bob up and down on the water trying to stay moored. Anna waits for her to continue.

I'm not even sure Marcus wants to be – probably wishes he had his own bachelor pad somewhere, like Chris.

Anna wraps her snood tight around her neck. Nancy thinks she looks pale.

And who is Chris? Anna asks.

You know, I told you, Nancy says, Marcus's right hand man. You don't want to know, disgusting specimen, fetid breath, teeth like a burnt pier. Anyway, he's probably planning his exit now. Marcus, I mean, in between seeing to patients on the slab. That's if he doesn't try to kill them first.

Leonora stares ahead, her feet swinging, swinging. Anna sighs.

You sound sour today, Anna says. He wouldn't…

He could. Just go, nothing stopping him, he could just up and leave at any time. A free man. He wouldn't have to face an unhappy wife and I wouldn't have to live with him facing an unhappy wife.

Look, where has this come from all of a sudden? I thought things were good between you two again.

Nancy runs her hand though Leonora's curls, transformed now from baby blonde to henna brown.

She broke me down, Anna says, as she does, chipping away until I gave in and bought her the dye. Naughty Leonora, taking advantage of her mother like that. A mean trick. She digs her teeth in and doesn't let go.

Leonora shrugs.

But why can't we stay here until it's dark? *Why*, Mummy?

That's why, Leo, don't argue, Anna says. In our day we didn't keep on like this. We wouldn't have dared, would we, Nancy?

Leonora rolls her eyes up to the empty sky.

It's cold now, Nancy says. Even the birds are hiding.

Leonora laughs. Nancy stares ahead. She tries to remember the last time she saw Anna laughing, which most likely was before Sebastian arrived on the scene. Nancy had often found herself wishing he had never existed. He had tried to have Leonora aborted, but Anna had refused. He disappeared at the first opportunity.

No, Marcus wouldn't do anything like that – not a bit of it, Anna says. He's in it for the long haul, that's obvious.

Leonora whistles. Anna squeezes Leonora's thigh.

Look at this, will you? She's getting pudgy. Her flesh is pinched by these tight jeans. I should get her exercising more.

Anna rubs her support down Nancy's arm.

Sorry to – look I know it's tricky, Anna says. How do you feel now? I mean about Georgia's news?

Nancy scrunches her fist, releases, scrunches, releases.

Marcus is pissed, Nancy says.

I asked about you, how do you feel? Was it a shock? She was nervous, wasn't she? She was fidgety all night before you arrived, now I think of it. I really think she didn't want you to know. That smile of hers, it takes over the whole room. She was squirming, wasn't she? When she told me I…

You knew?

Well.

Anna stops herself and looks over to the boats bobbing on the lake. Nancy pinches her leg.

You knew, Nancy says.

Anna manages a smile.

You don't have to contrive a smile for me and you don't have to worry, Nancy says. She hasn't ruined my life. Don't look at me like that, I don't need your sympathy. I know you'd never hurt me.

Leonora fidgets now and Anna responds again with a firm *no*.

Nancy had told Marcus once she thought Leonora must be lonely at home away from her friends with only Anna for company during the holidays – *And what does Leonora really have going with Sebastian, a few hours a week when he can fit her in? What had she been thinking back then? A fat, bald pseudo-intellectual. A journalist with as much warmth as an Icelandic summer. Anna should never have lowered herself like that. His own father married seven times, a warning bell if ever one clanged.*

A mother in a crimson duffel coat pushes a buggy in front of them.

One of the expensive, statement buggies, Anna says. I hate them. Saw them everywhere last summer in Richmond Park, but look at her with her baby. The mother looks around her, at her phone, everywhere other than where it matters.

Perhaps they're not so exciting after all, Nancy says.

Anna laughs.

Finally, Nancy says.

Ah, Anna says, now isn't he cute?

A mother pushes a buggy over the grass. Under a gingham blanket a toddler gazes at a lone goose strutting at the edge of the water. His tired-looking mother takes a photograph of him in front of the goose.

Nancy stares and stares.

Not a pang, no, she says to Anna, more like a tepid bandage wrapping itself around me, separating me. Playtime back in school: caring, cooking, organising, planning, fussing. Darting in the Wendy House at the first available opportunity – where else? Push a pram, set a table, small plastic plates, sizzle sausages for the husband, dead-eyed dolls waiting their turn. Is that okay for you, baby? Not too hot is it? Here, let me blow. Put a load on, pile the washing in the sink, run the carpet cleaner around and around, wag a finger. No, no, not now, I'm busy. Make sure you're back for your supper, now, you hear?

Anna rests her hand on Nancy's back. Leonora, tiring of adult conversation heads towards the lake clutching a bag of stale bread.

Look at her, Anna says. Her coordination's all wrong. She can't even throw properly.

Leonora turns around and heads back with an empty bread bag in her hand. Nancy watches Anna fasten the top button of Leonora's blue coat.

You make parenting look easier than I have any right to assume, she says. And you don't seem to need anybody, least of all a man. Sometimes I wonder what your needs are. You never complain.

There are things you don't know about, Anna says. That cheap bread, we only buy it for the ducks. Don't eat that stodge normally.

Mummy, what are you talking about? We had some for toast this morning with butter, remember?

Anna tugs at her daughter's hair. Leonora's eyes widen in confusion.

You can't keep up social appearances with her, Anna says. I've told you before about this, Leo.

The three of them turn their back on the water and the pedalos. In silence they make their way back towards the gate.

Can Nancy come back with us? Please, Mummy.

No, Leo, Anna says, it's a long way to Fulham from Bethnal Green and it's nearly rush hour.

Perlease Mummy. Nancy, you want to hear my song, don't you?

No Leo, really, it's a good idea we end it here, Anna says. No, now don't push it, we've had a good time.

Mum, perlease. Perlease. Mummy. Per…

A strong wind pushes Anna and Leonora towards the gates. Nancy turns back to see the light dimming over the water. Streaks of silver dance in the ripples. Knowing the alternative is to be home alone, Nancy agrees to go with them.

Outside, on the far side of the lawn, the shed door flaps open, shut, open, shut. He stares at the long grass through the blinds in the kitchen window. Another job he's been too busy to finish.

His eyelids flicker. Rising acid chunks threaten to jump out of his mouth. Turning to face the wall, he takes a moment to calm himself with a few deep breaths. With his right hand he pushes against the wall. He stops, his hands are shaking.

He attempts a star jump. Chris had shown him the slut-drop in the office, shimmying down the wall. *You've got to put all the weight on the knees. Tricky but that's the point. Good for the thigh muscles. You know where I first saw this, don't you? Some mad woman at the Notting Hill Carnival.*

Marcus tries it for himself but he only manages to shimmy a few inches before he gives up. There are tiny, stabbing pins in his knees. He thinks of William off playing golf, more dick-swinging and a chance to show off how much money he earned. Asabi had assumed she could go off on a break when she chose to.

Fired up again he attempts a few more star jumps. With the muscles in his legs quivering, he thinks ahead to his board meeting. It'll either make or break his career, but he never imagined in nineteen years of bullet-proof service this could ever happen to him.

Anna's hair is wrapped high in a turban and she looks at Nancy under heavy lids. Beside Anna, Leonora loiters in a black coat and a furry Russian hat. Nancy suspects Anna's more than ready for the handover.

Very cool, Nancy says to Leonora. The Slavic ice queen look suits you.

Nancy steps inside. Anna yanks off her turban, revealing glossy but damp hair in the sunlight. Nancy follows them both under the arch and through into the kitchen. With a tissue pulled from her pocket, Nancy mops the spilled milk from the table. Everything is still laid out from breakfast and will remain that way until Anna returns from work later.

So, Anna says, what you said on the phone – Marcus okay?

Not great.

Go on, Anna says.

He was – I've not seem him like that. I mean, you know he can be moody, but last night, well he was – it was brutal.

Nancy doesn't know whether to stop now before she cries or to go on. She's unsure how much to share with Anna. People, even close friends, were sometimes hard to trust with harsh truths.

It still feels unreal, Nancy says finally.

Do you think it's all the trouble with… you know? The girl?

Yeah, Nancy says. Oh, I don't know. I've worried too long through the night to go into this now. Do you mind?

She eyes the box of tissues by the kettle. A hand squeezes her shoulder.

Why don't we talk tonight when I get back from work?

Then I can give it the attention it deserves. Nancy nods in agreement.

Yes, she says, alright, it will do me good to forget for at least one afternoon.

Nancy clasps her phone in her hand and considers calling him to see if he's okay, but it would feel forced, wrong somehow.

Emerging from the tube, the sun blinds them through the clouds. Pointing in the direction of Centre Point, Nancy tells Leonora they're only minutes away from Marcus's hospital. Leonora's large blue eyes blink. Together they cross the footbridge that leads to the Tate and Leonora charges across.

Nancy watches her try to hop down the slope on the other side, but there are too many bodies to fight past. Instead, Leonora lumbers slowly down, humming to herself.

Inside the Tate, Nancy guides them through. They find themselves staring at a sculpture.

Plastic rabbits on sheets of bubble wrap? Leonora asks. I don't like it. The colours are horrible.

When they arrive in the Rothko space, Leonora pulls at Nancy's arm. When she sits next to Nancy on the white bench, swinging her legs, Nancy sighs.

I want to know, Nancy says, what you make of all this. Tell me which one you like the best and why.

Slowly, Leonora swivels her body around and takes in each of the paintings in turn. As she sucks on her lip, she spends a few seconds on each. She points to the one on the far right wall.

Why so? Nancy asks.

Because it's like a giant belly.

What?

Leonora smiles.

It makes me think of Sebastian. He wears a purple scarf. I mean it *feels* like Sebastian.

How so? Nancy asks.

It's bold and he's bold. It reminds me of a strong man.

Nancy smiles, but Leonora's blue eyes appear to turn grey in the dim light.

You don't have to feel sorry for me, Leonora says. He *is* my Dad.

A little sharp, Nancy thinks.

He is indeed, and I wasn't…

But he left us, Leonora says.

Nancy knows she has to tread carefully.

It's hard to know what to do when two people who love each other can't agree, Nancy says. He knew it wasn't right him and Mummy argued so much. That's all. Sometimes adults try and try.

Leonora shakes her head.

You don't know anything. You think you're smart but you don't know about any of this. If he left Mummy, he left me too.

Is that what Anna said to you?

No, well, kind of, dunno.

Then I wouldn't be so certain, Nancy says.

Leonora stares ahead.

But I am certain, Leonora says.

Certainty doesn't exist.

Hmm?

Not in a general sense, no. Everything can be argued and interpreted, absolutely everything. Apart from death and taxes.

This seems to please Leonora and she digs her elbow into Nancy's arm. Then she stands up to take a closer look at her painting.

But now I – now I'm not sure.

She sits down again.

They have that effect, Nancy says. You think you've figured the painting out, found the one you're most drawn to, but they're too strong to be understood, they like to trick you. It's like they're not of this world. Happens to me all the time. It's unusual to find somewhere like this in London, isn't it?

Leonora shrugs.

They're sick, she says.

Well, that's the power of good art. Rothko wanted you to feel how you're feeling now.

What do you mean? Leonora asks.

What I mean is he painted to please the person watching, to move them and elevate them in some way – get it?

No.

Leonora has heard enough and turns to face the door. Voices in the far distance rise and fall.

Yeah you do, Nancy says. Don't be awkward.

He sounds nice?

I wouldn't be too sure about that, Nancy says.

Why not?

Just because he's a good artist, doesn't make him a good – I mean he might have been, but we don't know that.

Leonora schleps by her side, staring down at her purple Doc Martins.

They're my moon boots, Leonora says. I can go anywhere in them, even to this weird place.

Weird?

Yeah, weird.

When they arrive in the café on the ground floor, Leonora chooses a table by the window.

The light through the glass highlights the pimples on Leonora's nose.

You're pretty enough through the puppy fat, Nancy says.

When they're settled at the table, Nancy tears the top of a sachet of sweetener. She looks down at her hands and notices fine crow's feet, a few more of them than before. Through the window, a couple push a buggy. She remembers Marcus the night before, tossing and turning. She couldn't get past the disconnect between them. Leonora taps her hand.

Will you be my agent when I'm older, Nancy, like you said you would? Can I come and live with you?

When did I say this?

I like you and I think Marcus is handsome. We'll have fun.

Leonora smiles, revealing milky-white teeth. Nancy wonders if her own teeth had ever been so white.

On the long white table next to them, twin boys in matching stripes sit erect in high chairs, one sleepy, the other sucking noisily on his finger. Leonora follows the line of Nancy's gaze.

You would make a good Mummy, wouldn't you, Nancy? How many children would you like? I'd like two, a boy and a girl. One of each. A girl to sing with, a boy to play football with.

Nancy had told June once that all around her are full lives and lives lived. She'd told her she'd like to throttle this pervading flatness, stretching before her like the Turbine Hall. A long grey walk to the exit, that's how it feels, and it scares her.

These nuts taste like hairy bums, Leonora says. Would you like one?

Leonora holds up her small pot but Nancy bats her hand away.

Anna's eyes are all taupe shadow and thick black liner. She moves around the kitchen clearing away plates and cutlery from breakfast and turns to her daughter.

Come on, Leo, you must have taken something in. So, tell me, what did you learn today?

Leonora scans the ceiling trying to find inspiration.

We went over the wobbly bridge, but it wasn't very wobbly.

Look Leo, I haven't got time for this. What did you see?

Stupid see-through plastic, sparkly bunnies. Lots of purple.

When she's finished clearing the plates, Anna sits hunched forward, squinting into a mirror and scrubbing away her make-up. Leonora spreads her arms out wide across the table and flops her head sideways.

She's just like the kids in my class, Anna says, they just don't – honestly, I've tried everything. All the tricks in the book. It means nothing. All the bullshit they write in manuals about how to control your class, and it's all abstract posturing, it doesn't work in practice. My dozy assistant Fleur, she's the laziest bitch in the world, thinks she's too good for the job. The head leaves it all up to me. I mean, really no support.

Nancy looks past Anna to a bowl of fresh vine tomatoes resting on the side of the sink. She wonders if Marcus is hungry.

Stay, Anna says. I'll cook. I'm going on a bit but I'll stop, promise.

But Nancy has to get away.

She kisses them both. Leonora's sad eyes peer at her from under her fringe. Her look says despite all her grumbling Leonora would have liked her to stay longer like she did in the old days. She hadn't tried to drag her up to her room like she used to do, but Nancy had often been able to sense her needs.

When Nancy steps out of the front door, she heads south. Approaching Mile End station, she once again finds herself staring at the District line map through the clear pocket of her purse. Peeling up the sleeve of her coat, she estimates it'll be nearly eight by the time she arrives. Georgia will still be at work, but she suspects Shiv will be there. She checks her phone. Another message from Tom.

So, let's get this right: you're saying it wasn't The Sundays. But you lie, you lie! WINK. I'll have to teach you a lesson. So, when are we meeting, at Barts again tommorow? Assuming your man's not going to be there after what happened. How do these things work, anyway? TELL ME. Or maybe we can meet later in the week in a park somewhere? Yeah, I know how that sounds, but where else?

When she arrives at Georgia's door, she peers through the stained glass window and rings the bell. Shiv moves barefoot into view. Through tired eyes, she sees his open shirt, his trademark smooth brown skin shiny under the ceiling lights. He opens the front door halfway and she takes this as an invitation to enter.

I didn't know you were coming today, he says in the kitchen, I would have tidied had I known. Did I forget something, Nancy? Georgia, she's not here.

They stand close together by the oak table. He edges back an inch.

But she'll be back in an hour or so, he says.

She knows him well enough to know she makes him nervous, much still unsaid between them. She can remember what it feels like to stroke his skin. She can remember what it feels like to touch the part of his torso, just above his hip, a place he loves to be touched. She had often wondered if Georgia knows the same spot.

Suddenly, aware of how needy she must look, how hazy

her intentions must look to him, she feels her cheeks turn hot. He turns his back on her and she eyes the length of his back, the same back that could just as well be made of clay than flesh.

Coffee, he says, I've only that pretentious Ethiopian stuff – Georgia's – okay with you?

When the coffee's made, he sits opposite her at the table. The room is smaller than her kitchen.. Light peppers through the tiny kitchen window above the sink. Birch trees overhang. The branches swing in the gloom as she digests the protracted seconds that threaten to swallow them up.

Is there something you want to say to me, Nancy?

No, I wouldn't say so.

She smiles to see him squirming. For a while, he sits biting his lower lip. His hands drum tensely on the table, inviting her to touch him, make the sound stop. Reaching her hands over the table towards him, their fingertips brush. This time she knows he'll understand her meaning and she doesn't wait, she rubs the web between his thumb and forefinger, the way she used to. She closes her eyes and keeps stroking.

Her arms feel light and her mouth dry. When she opens her eyes again she sees tears in his eyes. She wants to ask him: Does Georgia do this for you? Does she know what you like?

This is about Marcus, isn't it? He asks.

He hurts me, she says. He doesn't mean to but he does. It's his way, it's this impulse he has. Withholding and returning, always that. That's the pattern he's fallen into, that's the way it's always going to be. But you never did that to me.

Shiv squeezes her hand. He pulls back and the withdrawal stings her.

But he's your life now, he says. C'mon, you know this. I've been worried about you, to tell you the truth, we both have. Your mind always seems to be somewhere else these days.

He looks away.

I want to know what you're thinking, she says.

Really, he adds, if you think this is – I'm not the answer.

No.

But if it helps, he says, if it helps you.

She keeps her hand still. With her mind flying at this new sensation, she closes her eyes and waits for him to speak. When she opens them again he's standing. Slowly, he moves behind her and kneads her shoulders.

That's exactly the spot, she says.

She rests her head on his stomach, listening to distant sounds in his abdomen and she's close enough now to smell a milky darkness down there. More sunlight peeps through the window and creeps up his chest. He pulls away and walks towards the steps leading upstairs. When she's taken a minute to breathe, she follows him.

All is calm beyond the door. Having slept undisturbed through the night, she's refreshed and doesn't need anything, not even a glass of water. In the distance, she hears the sound of running water. There is a splashing sound. Guiltily, she closes her eyes and tries to clear her mind. A minute-or-so passes. Shiv's face appears, his eyes tired. The front door slams.

She shifts her weight on the sofa and heads into the bedroom.

The morning sun shines on the walls, glossing them. Speckles of lemon dot the foot of her white duvet. She can't recall if she'd washed it yesterday, but it smells clean. Lazily, she closes her eyes and keeps them closed until Shiv and Marcus's face merge into one. This new creature has Shiv's black eyes and Marcus's shaved head. Tom appears in front of this new face, but it's not the same Tom she saw in the hospital, it is the Tom of twenty years before. His long, auburn hair becomes a lion. She opens her eyes. Tugging the duvet tighter around herself, she wonders how much more she can take. It had been wrong, what happened, she'd whispered to Shiv in bed after. She'd been upset, should have gone for a long walk, or come home and cried like a good girl, instead of spreading her shit to those she cares about, just because she can.

She peels back her duvet and feels a cold sensation around her thighs. Standing in front of the wardrobe, she yanks open the doors. She scans the mess inside, wanting to clean, wanting to order. Furious now, she pulls neat piles of knitwear down from the shelves and throws them on the bed. Shiv will be discreet, he had told her as much. She feels a murmur in her chest, a flicker.

She sees Tom's auburn hair. It is after pub closing and they're holding hands. Together they walk up the steep path through the park. On the edge of the River Wye, a bird passes. It stops in front of them, making them slow down. Another chance to kiss. Around them, kids are drinking from cans and bottles. Two are naked, and they move up and down, up and down. The moon shines but it's not a full shine, it's as if it's glowing through cling film.

She heads into the bathroom. As she stands in front of the sink, she pulls floss from the toothbrush holder. When Shiv and her had been together, she'd fooled herself he hadn't looked at other women. She stares blankly at a large fly flailing and bashing against the pane. Shiv had enjoyed himself, relaxed into it, told her he'd thought of it often. He'd told her it was a strange feeling having her again, almost like happiness.

Tom's breath had been heavy as he'd leaned into her face. Slowly, he fumbled with her bra, turning it into a joke, pressing against her in his single bed. She could hear a clatter of steel pans in the kitchen downstairs. His mother had been down there in her olive sandals.

Gripping the edge of the sink now, she stares at her half-closed eyes, last night's black eye liner smudged just below her lashes. In bed with Shiv, there had been silence but she'd felt Georgia everywhere.

The doorbell trills against the floorboards. At the door, she feels a light draft around her ankles. She waits. A hand appears through the letterbox. She touches the hand, squeezing it tight. Slowly, she opens the door. There is a rub of fur across the top of her shoulder. Georgia touches her arm. She smells of pachouli.

Stand back, then, Georgia says, so I can get in. I thought I'd come around, you don't mind, do you? You called around last night?

Georgia leans back against the Welsh dresser in the hall.

He said you didn't seem yourself, she says.

Who?

Well, Shiv, of course.

She remembers Shiv's reassurances to her. Georgia would only spot the truth if she was looking for it – and why would she be looking for it? It wasn't the usual scenario: late back from work, smelling of another's perfume, lipstick on the collar.

Oh God, Nancy says.

What's up? Marcus. He's not here?

Marcus? Marcus.

Smooth chin, deep eyes, the one you're lucky to have?

Oh, him. He has his interview for the accident, she says slowly. He's there now preparing.

There?

Bart's of course, where do you think?

An accident, you say? Oh, they don't mess around these people, do they?

Together they head into the living room. Georgia flops

down on the sofa, cupping her knees, waiting for her older sister to speak. Her eyes scan and stab the air.

Is he nervous? Georgia asks.

He's angry with himself, Nancy says. He can't believe he allowed it to happen.

It's not like him to fuck up so royally?

Nancy bristles. She knows Georgia wouldn't know what was typical for him. Marcus never discussed work, not even with her. After a long, tiring day he only treated Nancy to a patchwork of grunts and sighs.

So, what's his plan? Does he have one?

Suddenly warm, Nancy removes her cardigan and drapes it on the arm of her chair.

He hasn't spoken of it at all. But I hope whatever happens he tells the truth.

Still, it was an accident, wasn't it? Georgia asks.

And warm turns to hot.

Meaning?

Meaning – Look, I can only go by what you told me. From what you were saying he wasn't exactly paying attention?

Nancy looks at her. Georgia ties and unties the bow on her blouse.

This is the first time this has happened and…

I know, but it's a responsible job. You know as well as I do, it's not like the jobs we do – *did*.

Marcus closes the door. The panel have just put him through the hardest test of his career. Every move of his during the operation had been questioned and tested. There had been five of them, two of them already known to him. With pertinent stares, they'd sat close together at a long desk in an airless room. Walsh's soulful eyes had been disbelieving. *This is unprecedented, Dr Connell. You were the last person I would have expected to be half-baked about your responsibilities.* The implication was clear, he'd let himself down, all of them down. Worst still, William had made a brief appearance. Pretending to have stumbled in the room by mistake, he'd whistled to himself, stopping only to deliver his cocky apologies and throw a sly glance in Marcus's direction. He found it impossible to concentrate after that.

Marcus had somehow ploughed on, told them his version of events as he believed them to be true. They'd made detailed notes. Time ticked on between the four walls, but an hour seemed as long as a day. When he was finally released, he was left alone to scratch his head and wonder. Shit happens, he'd muttered to Chris in the corridor, shit will always happen. He hated having to answer to everyone in the NHS. The pervading risk of human error couldn't be helped, it was a simple fact of hospital life – why then the punishment? Chris had tried to help, but he didn't understand how it all worked. He'd always kept himself in the background, never setting the hospital alight with his talent, nor attracting attention for the wrong reasons. Wise, probably.

Nancy appears before him in the corridor in smart boot cut jeans and a star patterned shirt.

You've made an effort, he says. A dab of peach lipstick, but it makes you look pale.

She clutches a foil parcel in her hands.

Everyone, he hisses. Everyone, for their own sakes should stay the hell away from me.

What's wrong, darling? I've just been with Georgia and…

Georgia just decided to turn up unannounced, then? Typical.

I hurried her out the door, she says. Couldn't bear to fake interest in the baby a second longer. So, how was it?

He takes lunch from her outstretched hand.

There's another round of questioning in a few days' time. They don't go easy on you these – look, I don't want to talk about it, alright? Feel my head.

It feels damp. Was it so bad?

He nods and turns his back on her. When he reaches the door of his office, he turns around and manages enough of a smile to make her happy again. She told Anna once she didn't understand why when she already had him, she ached for him. She'd never been able to figure it out.

She listens for a while. Chris's voice can be heard, loud but faltering. She turns her back on his office and makes her way to the west wing of the hospital. In Oncology, she looks anxiously around her but he's nowhere to be seen. She admonishes herself for thinking he would make all this effort for her when he had a sick wife to deal with.

Feeling listless, she presses the button to the lift. As she waits for the lift to ascend she feels a hand on her shoulder. She turns around.

You sounded upset, he says. Hard to tell with text, but call it masculine intuition.

Marcus, he's here, she says. Now. Not here exactly, in this room, but nearby. Sorry, jittery.

He smiles and pushes a piece of paper in her hand.

My other mobile number. I don't think I gave it to you last time we met.

She looks away from him and scans the faces of the patients around the edges of the room.

Your wife? Is she okay?

So-so. Look, it's just awkward using my other phone. My wife is cool with my female friends, but nothing escapes her.

And the lift she had summoned opens. She wants to stay, make arrangements, but instead she gives him an apologetic smile. Slowly, she enters the lift. The doors close quickly as she holds the paper in her hand.

Later, when she's back home, she wills herself to relax, and sets about knitting another blue square for her blanket. She enters into a trance, her safe place. When the square is done to her satisfaction, she stuffs the wool back in the basket. There is a text from Anna.

Sebastian's here. And he owes me one?

They meet between their two houses, in the relative quiet of Fitzrovia. As they sit together at a small brass table, dust blows in from the window, brutal, as if it was trying to expunge everyone. Intrigued to learn more about her news, Anna leans in.

I thought marriage would make me feel more secure about him, Nancy says. Why do you think it hasn't?

Anna smiles.

You never can tell. A ring, what difference does it make? Married or not, you're still individuals.

But it's a contract, Nancy says. I have him now, he's mine. He can't walk away just like that. At the same time, I just don't trust – I can't let myself.

Anna leans in further, straining to hear Nancy above the sound of a group of lads streaming over to the bar.

You know he won't walk away, Anna says. What is with you lately? He's committed to you. You're friends, that's the main thing. Look, I hope I'm not speaking out of turn – don't mean to sound flippant. I know all this has been a pain, but it's something you can work through, I'm sure of it. He's not the type to up and leave.

Anna strokes Nancy's arm. It soothes her. Scanning Anna's face for signs of irritation, she doesn't find any.

Poor Anna, she says. Always listening, always reasoning, and with your own shit to deal with. Perhaps that's it, Nancy says. I'm always fretting about an uncertain tomorrow, doesn't everyone?

Exactly, Anna says. Nobody knows what's going to happen.

Never mind, Nancy says. But it's hard.

Nancy pulls out the slip of paper Tom gave her, torn from the corner of a magazine.

Who does that messy handwriting belong to? Anna asks.

For the first time Nancy reads what is written. Lightly, Anna pulls it from her fingers.

You remember Tom, Nancy says. My first serious boyfriend back home?

Anna focuses on the piece of paper, frowns and shakes her head.

How…What…Why?

I found him.

Nancy leans back and waits for Anna to speak.

You don't have to look so smug about it, Nancy.

I'm not.

Oh, sure.

He'd been waiting for me. That's how it felt.

Anna stirs her gin with a straw. She blinks and blinks again.

Bullcrap. You went looking for him.

No. I – no – well, maybe.

You want to see him again, is that what you're saying? Because I thought it ended badly between you two back then. He was – now I can't – have I got this right? He was something of a mystery. He was *different.* I'm remembering that right, aren't I?

But lately he's been on my mind. Suddenly, I don't feel like talking to you about this.

Oh please. Why?

I'm allowed to, aren't I, check in with an old flame, no law against it. I'd forgotten all about him, that's all. That is, until that session with June.

June?

My therapist. Remember, I told you, we're going to therapy now. Anyway, Marcus was working late – again – so I went on my own. It took me a while to remember his name after that therapy session – can you believe that? Is Tom so hard to forget? I tried and tried, but I just couldn't remember.

You mentioned him in therapy? Anna asks.

Nervously, Nancy sips her red wine. She wipes her lips with a tissue.

It just sort of came out of the blue. We were talking about Julia and – and she was – she was rude to him. We were talking about Julia, that's all.

Right?

Anna flicks her straw at Nancy. Nancy smiles.

Go on, then, Nancy says. Treat me to some of that amateur psychology of yours.

Thank you. It's not so amateur. I did that long course at Birbeck, remember?

Sorry.

Anna leans back and Nancy waits. There is a burning sensation in her stomach. She sips more wine and it tastes sharp. Carefully, she puts down her glass.

He reminds you of a time when life was simple, Anna says, when you had your whole life ahead of you. And I guess a future love was part of that childish plan. But now it's different. A more realistic future, and it's that you'll be wise to plan for. Maybe an even more exciting future you can't imagine yet is just around the corner that doesn't include a man at all. And if you want my advice –

No, I don't.

Forget about Tom.

Would it be so bad to just have a harmless drink? I *am* curious.

Okay, then consider this: how would you feel if he bought his wife along with him? Because it seems to me what you really want is to see him alone. Now, go on, admit it.

Nancy shrugs, but a conspiratorial smile creeps up Anna's face. Anna looks at her a beat too long.

Who said he was married?

You did, with your guilty smile. Just be careful is all I'm saying.

Asabi addresses them around the meeting table. He fixes on her, imagining her favourite bra under her uniform, taupe lace. Her face looks bare but there's a dark shine to her cheeks and lips. He liked how she was subtle with her make-up. He often enjoyed the way she tried to fool everyone with the illusion she was too clever to bother with a beauty routine. But she did bother. He'd been married long enough to know.

As she listens to Walsh speak, she smooths down the tip of her fringe and looks up coyly. Carefully, Marcus slides the lid back on his pen. His second and final interview is due to start in under fifteen minutes and if it goes like he thinks it's going to go, it may well be his last.

The previous day, he'd had to meet with the parents of the dead girl to explain to them fully what had happened. Later in the pub with Chris he'd described their hollowed-out faces. The hardest thing I've ever had to do, he'd said. What could I say? What happened, doctor? I see. Okay, yes I see. Thank you, doctor, for all you've done. Christ, their conciliatory understanding. The humble victims cow-towing to me.

One by one they file out of the meeting room, but he stays rooted to his seat. To his surprise Asabi stays too. With just the two of them, he waits for her to speak. He wants her more than he can remember. Without thinking, he rises out of his seat and goes to her. She stands and they kiss. It feels good, soft and urgent. He changes his mind. Pulling back from her, he knows he has to get as far away as possible.

What's wrong, Marcus?

You must have heard? Of course you fucking have. You were there – at least you should have been.

I'm sorry, Dr Connell?

The blankness in her face fires him up with jealousy, her easy role, no sense of ultimate responsibility. He would take a pay cut in a heartbeat to be in her position. He knows she'll have no idea about investigative procedures yet – not a whiff. Her simple existence as a trainee anaesthetist nurse, polished, pulled out of college a few days a week and thrust into the world of theatre.

You have no idea? He asks.

I have no idea what you're insinuating unless you tell me.

Carefully, he sits back down.

So now the formal college speak, he says. Let it drop for a moment. The girl, stupid, I'm under investigation.

He taps out a drum roll on the table.

The girl who died last week?

You're quite brilliant.

Oh, I see.

She waits, but he, as he's often done, enjoys taunting her with silence. She looks past his head and out of the fifth floor window. She smooths her hair and walks past him to the door.

And my essay, did you read it yet?

He wants to laugh.

You know, he says, sometimes I'm endeared by your self-absorption. You think you're such a vital cog in the wheel. You have no idea how hard it is for me to have gotten this far in my career.

She swings the door open wide and Chris blusters in.

Pint later, doc? I think you're going to need one, yes?

Marcus nods. Chris leaves satisfied and Asabi shakes her head.

Such a fool, she says, he gets worse, creeps me out.

He ignores this. He's heard it too many times from the other staff in the hospital. Instead, he rummages in his bag and pulls out her dog-eared essay. He hands it back to her.

I think you should give this to Chris to read, he says. I'm much too busy.

As she leaves, there's steel in her smile and it worries him.

Alone on the tenth floor, he paces the locker room.

Just get through this and everything will be okay, Chris had told him. You can handle this. Just use your brain. Plan man, plan.

And he's summoned.

The faces that wait for him are the same ones that questioned him before. As they wait for him to settle in his chair, they examine him as if he were an unfamiliar germ under the microscope. They had just as well be featureless, he can't take them in.

A woman with short, thin hair introduces the procedure for the session. She announces there will be a few brief questions and he is able to glimpse the questions running down to the foot of the page.

Sitting upright, ready for action, he rests his nervous hands on his lap. The thin-haired woman slowly opens her file. The air stills. Asabi's name is mentioned. His breath falters, he hadn't thought of that. She's called in from waiting outside the door. Carefully, she enters and takes the chair at his side, waiting with her face in neutral for their questions.

Yes, Asabi says finally, that's exactly how it was. I told Dr Connell I was going for my break. He said fine, take your time.

The woman with the thin hair looks over the rim of her glasses.

Is this true, Dr Connell?

No, I wouldn't say so. I don't recall Asabi mentioning she was going on a break.

Sorry? You did say it Marc – Dr Connell, Asabi says. You may have been distracted but you definitely said those words. Those exact words.

Asabi looks to the line of faces as if expecting their support.

Because how was I to know he wasn't listening? After all, what would you do? What would you have done in my position? If he said it was okay to go, then I have to assume it was okay for me to go.

The woman with thin hair nods.

And did you notice anything about Dr Connell's behaviour that was unusual that day?

There is a meaningful silence, Marcus's throat tightens. Asabi's eyes widen.

I thought at the time he was texting a lot. In fact, so much so I recall I was going to ask him if he was feeling okay. But I don't like to get involved in petty domestics. Not my place to interfere. I like to keep it professional, as I'm sure you understand.

Walsh scribbles furiously in his notepad.

And how often was he texting? Walsh asks.

Well, if I'm honest – and I have to be honest, don't I? Every time I glanced over. Like I say, I was going to say something but I – I'm sure you can appreciate I'm still a junior. And as a junior, I'm learning from his example.

Marcus's head hurts. He holds his breath for a second or two, hoping this will help. Slowly, he rubs the stubble on his head. Any movement would be better than none at all. Asabi glances at him. He attempts a smile that says *I've underestimated you, this is quite a performance*, but quickly drops his smile.

Have you anything to add, Dr Connell? Walsh asks. Because that's a serious allegation you're making there, miss.

The woman with thin hair leans back, eyes pin-sharp and grey.

I say she's not remembering it clearly enough, that's all, Marcus says. Easily done, I guess. But she's forgetting something important.

Oh, Walsh says.

The woman's eyes adjust themselves from suspicious to curious.

We were alone. There were no other witnesses. As it happens, it's her words against mine.

He can still hear the sound of the door hinge creaking, the moment when Asabi had exited the room, full and satisfied. Chris looks up from his pint and smiles, his two front teeth matching the brown swirls on the carpet. Marcus listens as Chris imparts his observations.

Always thought she was a schemer, Chris says. You know I've been watching her. I've been watching how she is with you. Suspended, eh? Man, that's tough. Really bloody tough. So, she fucked you over, then, tried to warn you, didn't I?

Whatever her agenda had been, he says, I didn't deserve it. Have you read her essay?

What essay?

I told her to give it to you to read. Do this, do that, those sad cow eyes. But she's no idea, it's nothing personal, any of this. Christ, to think what I've had on my plate.

Making a hook with his right hand, Chris pokes his finger through. Marcus ignores this and looks away.

I was just trying to do my job, Marcus says. Juggling all the shit I have to deal with – and not just at work.

I know that, Chris says. I have eyes and ears but Asabi's an attractive woman and you didn't make it clear enough to her. Women don't like being ignored. Fatal error, fatal error. None of *this* forthcoming, was there? So, what did she do? She took great delight in revenge.

Marcus shakes his head.

You have to hand it to her, Chris says. Dangerous game, getting involved with these trainees.

I didn't get…

If you will insist on leading these women on, you get punished one way or…

Lead her on, is that what you're after saying? The irony! I can barely muster the energy to fuck my own wife.

The Iranian doctor in Oncology? Chris asks. You must have seen her. Having an affair for sure. Some grey-haired accountant. He's been spotted picking her up in the hospital car park in his red sports car.

Marcus listens. He nods in all the right places, but his mind spins with thoughts of Nancy.

I have no idea yet how I'm going to break the news of my suspension, Marcus says. And I miss her income. Loved her coming home in her sharp suits.

I'll bet.

They're all laid out on the bed in the spare room gathering dust. It's been six months now and she's changing before my eyes. But those suits, that pinstriped one from Saville Row. I loved her coming home after a long day with a difficult client. Now though, she's so – pissing her life away, never realised before.

What will you do with your time now?

No idea. Go out of my mind.

Chris looks at him with a new hardness he hasn't seen before.

Oh pity, Chris says. You can do all the stuff you want to do. You can go cycling on those shiny new bicycle lanes. No more trying to cram all you want to do in at the weekends.

Unexpectedly, Marcus feels a new sensation: he feels like talking to Chris, and talking properly, not about Chris's Honda bikes or the growing helmet collection he keeps in the conservatory, but about the big subjects of life, love and loss. But it's a risky game. He wants to confide, but he knows he'll never do it, show his vulnerability, giving him ammunition to use at a later date.

You know the others turned against you long before all this?

Where the hell has this come from? Marcus asks.

Come on, do I have to spell it out to you?

You already have.

You've been getting too big for your boots.

Marcus grips his empty pint glass and waits.

You've had a meteoric rise, but you've forgotten to be nice to all those people who supported you, who championed you when you started here and didn't know what the hell was going on. There was a time – and I remember it well – when you didn't have a single ally. You think people forget?

Ah, come…

You think they haven't noticed how you are with Asabi? You've become…

Not an affair, you fool.

Take it from me.

No you misunder… nothing dangerous like that.

Okay, let's change the subject, but don't play the innocent card.

Marcus has heard enough.

Another hour in your company would completely obliterate my already disastrous day, Marcus says, as well as my sanity.

With a new heaviness, Marcus rises out of his seat. He could sleep for a thousand years, he tells him. Slowly, he ties his hood tightly around his face, brushes clumsily past a drunk couple snogging at the bar, and walks out into the rain.

Nancy waits. A seagull swoops overhead and glides the full length of the park. When it's out of sight, she gazes at the old oak tree. The names *Tallulah* and *Amelie* are scratched inside a love heart. A young man in a flat cap passes by with his dog, a whippet. Nancy thinks the dog's face looks unbearably sad. She checks her watch.

There's a tightness in her abdomen and this time a cramping. Carefully, with a tissue pulled from her bag, she scrapes damp mud from her shoe and sighs from deep inside herself. When she looks up again she sees him through the trees. At first he doesn't appear to see her. Huddling his chin inside his woollen scarf, his orange trainers tread towards her. He smiles at her and settles by her side. Absent-mindedly, she strokes her thighs that are rooted to the wooden slats of the bench, willing herself to stay calm.

Am I late? He asks.

Yeah, a bit, but no matter. Actually, I'm early.

Slowly, he crosses his legs, pointing them towards Tallulah and Amelie and away from her. He yawns loudly. She sees his perfect white teeth are the still same. She laughs but he sighs and it jolts her.

So, what is it? He asks.

Your hair, your body, it's weird how much you've changed. I mean, you've changed, but your teeth?

My teeth? What about them?

She looks at her lap and pinches her thigh to stop herself from rambling. The muddy ground slants down in the direction of the river. For a second, it makes her feel as if she's falling.

So why did you want to meet here?

I thought you'd like it, she says. It's the best kept park in London.

Okay.

She shows him the scrap of paper he'd handed to her in the hospital.

Well, yeah okay, I'd forgotten I'd said I'd come to your part of town. Was just throwing something out there.

What if she were here? She asks herself? The conversation would be different somehow. It would be lighter and more polite. That might be nice. Nicer than this. Sometimes I wonder what you remember about me. The smell of musky amber in my hair? Smoke on the lapel of my green velvet jacket? She puffs out a breath that clouds in the cold.

Is your wife going to be okay? She asks.

Who, Ange? Oh, right.

For a moment or two, there's silence.

She's not my wife. As good as – but no.

She looks at him and sees in his eyes the reason for his surliness. He looks on the verge of tears.

I'm really very – I'm so sorry.

He digs the heels of his orange trainers down into the mud.

It sucks. I'm sick of that stinking place, that fucked up disease. You'd think they would have found some answers by now? All that money ploughed into research, but…

Do you have any children of your own?

He snorts, and taking that as a no, she sits back.

I guess I've been thinking about the past a lot lately, he says. And if I'm honest with myself, that's why I wanted to meet when you got in touch.

He turns to face her, but only fleetingly.

Me too, she says, thinking about the past, obviously. I'm trying to get over something too.

Oh?

I've lost something special. I guess you could say…

Say what?

Lately, there's been a dark pit and I haven't been able to climb out of it. Nobody can tell me what's wrong with me.

Oh, I see.

Except you don't, nobody does.

The hands resting on her lap are shaking. She hadn't been expecting silence. Anna had been right. Stupid, dangerous nostalgia, no good will come of it.

His phone bleeps and he pulls it from his pocket.

I really do have to be going now, he says, I'm sorry I can't stay longer. She needs me at home.

He glances shyly at her, a new softness in his smile.

But we can do this again – if you'd like to. It's lonely all this sitting around and waiting and drumming my fingers.

She watches him slope down the path towards the gate and hopes he won't turn around to see the relief in her face.

Holding his crotch in one hand, and jiggling his key in the lock with the other, he wishes he'd taken Chris's advice and used the toilet before leaving the pub. When the door opens and he's inside, he tries to wrench the trainers from his feet. Just before his bladder explodes, he bursts into the bathroom and lifts the toilet lid. Hovering with his trousers gathered around his ankles, he listens. Nothing, not even a pipe creaking. For London, the place was quiet – too quiet he'd often complained to whoever would listen. The neighbours were probably involved in some kind of criminal activity. A few corpses under their patios. Quiet ones are the worst.

After he's relieved himself, he grabs a tube of toothpaste to help him to sober up. Dabbing some toothpaste onto his brush, he looks back at his grey reflection and wonders again about his neighbours.

Blake had moved in around the same time as him and Nancy, which might have made them friends. Nancy had told him Blake and his wife often had friends around, friends with other noisy toddlers,

He had long suspected Blake was a writer. He worked from home most of the time and lately he'd taken to drinking fresh coffee on the lawn. He could be a journalist or a novelist, but he'd never bothered to ask.

Keeping to themselves, Marcus had often complained to Nancy he felt they were different to other couples. There were outsiders – outsiders even in the patchwork oddity of London.

In the kitchen, he hovers a pint glass under the cold tap. Changing his mind, he opens the fridge for a beer. He pulls the ring and sighs with pleasure to hear the hissing sound. So damn quiet, he said to Nancy last night. Did anyone know their neighbours in London?

Slumping back against the fridge door, he surveys the scene. The work surfaces, dirty and uneven, need to be wiped but he's tired. He'd like to bleach every fleck and the spaces in between. Tomorrow, he decides, if Nancy won't, he'll do it himself. Drowsily, he takes a glug of lager and pours the remainder down the sink. He decides he doesn't need any more complications. His wife and her relationship with Georgia was one.

He remembers when he had first met Georgia, he had disliked her instantly. She wasn't to be trusted, and he recognised it, the mirror effect. Like him, Georgia could be cynical and controlling. Not like the sister he'd wanted to marry.

He sluices the lager away in the middle section of the sink and rubs some warmth into his cheeks. Piece by piece, he forms the memories of the past ten years into an overview. Nancy had always been compliant. Opposites attract, Shelagh had told him once. But he wished he didn't have to tolerate her family, her friends.

His head is heavy with it all. He pulls open the dishwasher door, puts another tab in to freshen the festering load that has been resting there for days, and turns the dial. Lazily, he stares at the black porcelain cat on the windowsill. Nancy might like a cat, he'd told Chris in the pub. They weren't on her radar, but that was only because she'd never thought about them.

He misses pets. As a kid, he'd had them: a dog with three legs, a goldfish for two weeks until it had suffocated, a gerbil that ate its own baby. Maybe that's all it would take, he'd told Chris, something for her to look after, a focus outside of herself.

He stretches his arms up and thumps the ceiling. At least, he concedes, his life had been simpler than Chris's. Yet there was something about him he admired. He had values. He believed in the NHS and everything it stood for – every understaffed, under-resourced, rapidly-shrinking inch of it.

He grabs a glass of water and heads into the living room where he surveys Nancy's choice of soft furnishings. Lately, the only colour he sees is orange.

He slumps down on the sofa and stairs up at the ceiling. He could invite his colleagues over. Show them he's not the jumped up arse they all think he is, but he bats away the thought. Reaching into his pocket, he pulls out two tabs of codeine and swallows them down. He pulls out his phone. Asabi answers, sounding sleepy.

That old cliché of a woman spurned, he hisses. Because what's worse than making a pass at a woman? Not making a pass at one. Chris had relayed that little titbit – or had it been Frank? But what if you'd known I'd been banging my head against the wall wanting to fuck you? Would that have made a difference? Ifs, ifs and more ifs. It's too late now. But the boredom, the routine, the way you looked up to me and the power. So easy for me to exert, so tempting for you to fall for. A student, the one who wants to learn, and every girl wants a doctor, right? Even an NHS one.

She hangs up and he sighs. Sensing it will be dark soon, he moves to the window. The manicured bushes lining the street are endless. Slowly, the sky turns a brilliant red and he wonders where his wife is. Lately it felt to him as if they were roommates, not a married couple. Everything needed to be paid for. Doctors used to be rich and lived in big houses. Not the ones he knows. Not him.

As he stares out the window at the brilliant red, his left hand feels its way over to the laptop. Hovering the mouse over his last listen, he closes his eyes. Bach's phrases repeat and slide into each other. Not people like him. Not the vocational doctors.

The sky is a brilliant red. Nancy drifts past manicured lawns and families gathered around oak tables, visible through large bay windows. Fulham's unending streets are calm in the twilight. Anna walks by her side.

I wonder, Nancy says, what he had been thinking, taking his mind off the job. Because with a job, any job, concentration is all. It's one place where you aren't allowed leverage to daydream. That's why I had to leave the bank, until I knew other people's money could be safe from my wandering mind. More problems to add to an already overflowing pot. And Georgia. Wicked, the things he says about her. So insidious, his attitude, spreading his poison. He doesn't understand her.

When Anna has kissed her goodbye and she reaches the front door, she rings the bell. He doesn't answer. Slowly, she twists her key in the lock, pushes open the door, and so as not to wake him closes it carefully behind her. Alone in the living room, she pulls her mobile from her bag and scrolls down to the letter T. She'd wanted to as soon as he'd said goodbye in the park. With a hushed voice, she calls and leaves a message for him to meet her the following day. The same place, the same time, and the same bench.

With more determination than she's been able to muster for a while, she hauls herself up from the cushions scattered on the sofa. Faintly she recalls Marcus whisper to her earlier. He was heading out for a run.

She stands in front of the bathroom mirror. The light is dull outside and her newly washed face is pale. Slowly, she rubs some rose cream into the apples of her cheeks.

Carefully, she undresses, pulls off her jeans and throws them in the linen basket. Entering the bedroom, she selects a fresh pair of jeans from the drawer. She pulls them on but they feel tight, pinching her gut. Looking in the mirror sideways, she is aware her to-do list is expanding along with her girth.

When she's left the house she makes her way to the park, but instead of taking the District Line, she walks. As she makes her way down the road, she looks at her lemon running shoes. With every step the reality of seeing Tom again grows nearer, and the feeling excites her.

She remembers The Sundays sang mournfully on his record player.

Arriving in the park, she walks towards Tallulah and Amelie trapped forever inside a love heart. She tells herself this time she'll listen to him. She won't interrupt, won't scare him off again, will focus only on him.

He walks towards her, his scarf as multi-coloured as the leaves at his feet. Closer now, so close she can see the blueness of his lips, she watches him flex his fingers in front of him. He manages a smile and sits by her side.

I'm so grateful you're smiling, she says, I could kiss you.

There's a lot I want to tell you, he says.

Me first, she says. I mean, it's been on my mind since seeing you at Bart's last week. But it seemed too soon yesterday and…

It's about my partner, Ange, he says, agitated. Come with me. Let's take a walk to Brompton cemetery. It's a good twenty minutes from here. There's something I want to show you.

She does as he says. Walking behind him, she tracks the marks of his soles in the mud, a size nine. The same shoe size as Marcus. They head out of the gate and east along the trunk road. The buildings look soft and sad under the winter-grey sky. At a junction, he stops to peer in the window of a hardware store. They arrive at the cemetery gates and enter in silence. Quickening his pace, he heads up the long path that seems endless. There are yells and grunts from the football pitch beyond the west wall. Above her is the distant crow of a blackbird. He slows to take a call on his phone.

The cheers from the football pitch grow louder. The walkway stretches on. They're the only ones heading in the direction of the central monument. Ahead of her, he mumbles what sound like orders. He sounds clipped with whoever he's speaking to.

A squirrel flits past and rests on a gravestone, its quick eyes dart in her direction and then all around him. Blocks of fading light remind her the short, winter day is already planning its exit and she buttons up her duffel coat. A neon badge falls. She'd hadn't realised it was still fastened under the collar. Bending down to pick it up, she sees him stop and spin around.

Tell me, Nancy. What *is* the meaning of life?

She catches up and stands next to him. His eyes scan a glut of mossy and overgrown gravestones.

Take these Celtic crosses: they've been here for centuries. And they'll be here long after we're cold in the ground too. Do you ever stop to think what your headstone will say, Nancy? Do you? I do all the time.

No, I can't say I…

When it's my turn, I wonder if I should choose something witty – pithy even. See, I told you I was ill. Like Spike Milligan? Why not. Better than solemn. Let's face it, what do any of us matter, anyway? People think their lives are important but I'm not so sure they are.

He takes a right and quickens again. Light breaking through a cloud reveals a small bald patch on the back of his head. She surprises herself how much she wants to touch it, the stamp of time passing. He stops again. This time, he rests his hand on something, a black marble gravestone.

So here we are, he says.

Here we are?

A small bunch of withered bluebells rest by the stone. Tom purses his lips together. She waits. He grabs the chipped gravestone and shakes it.

Still doing okay, isn't it? He asks.

What is? What are we doing?

She sees his hand is shaking as he licks his index finger and scrubs away at the dirt on the marble. First the letter N is revealed. He rubs some more. The date is 1994.

This, he says, this is what I wanted to show you.

Marcus steps down from his bike and nods to Blake in his car, testing his headlights. He'd often wondered why he spent so much time outside in the blistering cold when he has a wife and kid at home. There must be a story there somewhere. It was the same with all the neighbours, secret stories, comings and goings in the darkness, none of your business. Blake nods back, but he detects a hint of hostility behind his eyes.

He wipes sweat from his forehead and battles a key in the lock. When he is safely inside, he heads into the kitchen, opens the fridge, peers inside and slams it again. He tries the cupboards. First he selects a can of tomatoes, pulls back the ring and waits for the hob to heat itself. While he waits for his food he rubs his thighs and grips his crotch. The last time he had attempted to please his wife, she had been like a doll, dead.

He slops the tomato on to some stale bread, heads into the bedroom, plumps the cushions and relaxes back with the plate resting on his knees. At his feet is a copy of *Cycling Monthly,* but he is not in the mood for reading.

Casually, he turns on the remote, but finding nothing of interest, he flicks through the channels at speed. In exasperation, he throws the remote at the wall. The batteries roll across the carpet and buffer against the door. He stabs a tomato with his fork.

His recent ennui made for a heady cocktail. His brain, he suspected, was beginning to dribble slowly and irrevocably out of his ears. He had yet to complete his research paper. He could at least try if he were able to concentrate. Perhaps most worrying of all, there was his growing disinterest in sex. The big red warning light if ever there was one, Chris had told him once. Hugely disorientating.

He recalls Saturday night.

She had propped herself up in bed facing him, her nipples purple under the red lamp. That night he had been filled with love but also with guilt, admiring her appeal, her aestheticism, but being too tired to show her. He'd dabbed her nipple with his finger. As her back arched, it happened, he'd froze. Instead of trying to bring her to the conclusion she deserved, he'd ordered her to roll over, her back to him. Slowly, he ran his hand across her belly. So different, so depressingly at odds with how he used to be.

A roar from the stadium makes her head spin. As the light fades from twilight to black it transforms the trees. She thinks they look powerful, as if they know the secrets of the dead they guard over. She checks her watch for the third time in as many minutes and reminds him the gates will be closing soon to keep the drunks out.

Tom looks at her, waiting. Stooped now, he looks for a reaction, anything she can give.

Nancy, she says. Who is Nancy? I don't understand.

He grips the gravestone tightly – so tightly the skin around his knuckles is as pale as the moon peeping through thunderous clouds.

I'll tell you, he says.

But are you? Are you going to tell me, or are we just going to stay here like this? We really should get going. They'll be locking the gates soon and I –

Ange and me, we met at Oxford. So, I guess that's why I stopped writing to you.

But that was all that so long ago. What's this all about, tell me?

Ange got pregnant, is what I want to tell you. No wait, listen to me. It was terrible timing. Only nineteen. Unheard of to be a parent at that age. Certainly not in the circles we moved in. All the Henrys, Camillas and Candidas.

And?

I didn't have anything to offer her, not then. But she went ahead and had the baby anyway. I couldn't stop her, could I? The baby was never satisfied. We got used to it, all the crying and sleepless nights, but one night we just couldn't stand it, I suppose it broke us in the end. We left her with Ange's sister. We needed to get out just for a pint, the two of us, nothing drastic, just a change of scene and air. Been a while. Oh God, I don't know why I'm going on like this, It wasn't Gill's fault – Gill, her sister. But when we got back in the early hours, well, Gill was beside herself. The baby was…

Dead, she whispers.

The coroner delivered a cot death verdict, and we buried her but as the years rolled on, neither of us could…

Could face trying again?

She scrambles around internally for reassurances, but she doesn't know what to say. Finally, he lets go of the stone.

So, I wasn't sure whether to mention it to you. I thought about it yesterday, but I didn't want to scare you or anything. Look, she was a happy kind of soul. Her curls.

Sadly, he rubs his fingers over the lettering.

I suppose it's just a name, he says. Doesn't mean anything. She existed, had a family, a birth certificate, parents who loved her and…

It was a life all the same, she says.

I've always liked the name Nancy.

Together they walk down the path towards the exit. When they reach the gate, a stern-faced keeper approaches shaking his keys. It is then Tom hugs her and she doesn't stop watching him until he's out of the gate and out of sight.

Heading home, she considers how different it all used to be, everything, absolutely everything. He was fragile. Where before he had strong muscles and thick curls, he was now pushed around by life in the same way everyone was. The rolling iron ball of experience had flattened him, flattened them all.

She steps up her pace now. She sees a silver letterbox and in the bowels of the house, she hears the sound of a piano playing. Für Elise but the pacing is too fast. Marcus will be back home wondering what's happened to her…

Turning into her road, Shiv's dark body flashes through her mind but she blinks him away – a moment of weakness, that's all. And Georgia. The one everyone struggles to fathom. The sister they're all afraid of, the one she trips over herself trying to please. But why?

She speeds up and reaches the door. Under the buzz of the street lights, she can hear Bach playing, and it's then she sees him there, silhouetted at the window. Slowly, she opens the door and steps inside. How long, she wonders, has he been stood there? When she walks in, she sees his eyes are glazed, as if he's taken something. He tells her everything.

Oh, it's not so bad, he tells her. At least now I'll have time to think.

Alone in bed, she slides under the duvet and waits for him to finish up in the bathroom. He takes his time and she closes her eyes. The sound of gushing water stops. The next sound she hears is the door of the spare room clicking shut.

A bauble the size of her fist rolls across the floor. She watches it roll to a stop by the television. Slowly, she bends down and hangs it back on the tree.

She switches the flashing tree lights off, a present from

Shelagh, and heads into the hall. There, she selects her favourite red coat with the large buttons from the hook. She knows she needs to be out today, busying herself – out of the house in the buffering cold, away from him.

She rides the number 11 bus into town, her favourite route. With sleepy eyes, she gazes at Big Ben, Westminster Abbey and finally, Trafalgar Square. The Strand is busy with Christmas shoppers; it makes her head ache but she smiles remembering something Anna had told her once. People should be fitted with brake lights. There should be a fast lane for people like them and a slow lane for people like her. Today, she'd be happy to take the slow lane.

She arrives at Somerset House to find Anna and Leonora waiting for her. Leonora claps her huge, sheepskin mittens together. Anna's eyes dart around the changing room, wondering what the system is, where she can pick up her boots, what to do with them when she has them. Leonora hands over their tickets and they change into their skates. On the ice, Nancy and Anna grip tightly onto the sides. Leonora shoots off.

So this is why mad bitches like us come ice-skating, Anna says. Just so we can make fools of ourselves.

For a second time, Leonora whizzes past them. Anna swipes to grab her coat tail, but she misses and swipes the air instead. Leonora doesn't look back.

Would you believe she's only been once before? Anna says. She makes me sick. I suppose I should be glad. At least I've found something to keep her active, something she's good at.

With her arms shaking, Nancy lets go of the side but it's only seconds until she falls. Anna wobbles hauling her up. With Nancy's fear of failure now gone, she tries again. This time she manages a few seconds of fearful motion before she falls again. Leonora skates in broken circles around her.

Take my hand if you like, Leonora says. I'll show you. See, you're doing it! Does Marcus skate? Bet he'd be good at it, good at everything, isn't he? And he'd know what to do if someone fell over and hurt himself, wouldn't he?

This is so good it should make your head spin. We bought it in Sicily last year.

Shiv unwraps the bottle and slams it on the pine worktop. Georgia rises to fetch the shot glasses from the freezer. Nancy risks a glance at Marcus, slouched and surly on his stool at the breakfast bar.

I'm relieved you're behaving yourself, she whispers, perching on the stool next to him. Herculean of you to hold your tongue all through Georgia's Sicily lecture.

A special occasion? Georgia asks Shiv.

Does it have to be? Shiv asks. Just thought I'd share. That's what people do, isn't it?

Nancy slides her arms around Marcus's waist.

Oh, here we go, Marcus says. And did you see? He had a whole bottle of red to himself. That steak'll be sluicing around in that expanding gut of his.

When Georgia and Shiv turn their backs on them, she nudges him. Georgia faces her and hands her a glass. Over by the fridge, Shiv rolls up his shirt sleeve and pulls out the cork, smirking at the popping sound. He approaches and pours them each a drop. Nancy stares down at her limoncello and takes a sip.

Tastes amazing, she says quietly, like lemon sherbert.

This was the highlight of our holiday, Shiv says.. That and the prune port, of course. But we're not sharing that, are we Georgia?

Marcus swallows his down with one tilt of the head.

Not bad, he says.

Nice, Shiv says.

Nancy sighs. Growing fidgety, she slips her heels back on and eyes the clock above the cooker.

Okay, Shiv, Marcus says. Not everyone's mad enough to spend £50 on a bottle of liqueur.

I suppose you'll want to be going, Georgia says, hauling herself out of her seat. Nancy wants to laugh. She's barely showing yet.

So I'll get you an Uber, Georgia says. Cheaper than flagging one down.

Shiv looks at Nancy. She detects a hint of malice in his smile, but she hopes she's wrong. She flashes him a look that is a distinct warning.

Marcus stifles a belch as he watches his wife pull nervously at her dress. A minute or two passes before she leaves the room to join her sister in the hall. Nervous now, Shiv offers him another drop of liqueur.

I was just sat here wondering, Marcus says, what could be behind your sickly smile.

Ignoring him, Shiv rolls the liqueur around his tongue and swallows.

So, just me and you here, Shiv says. How is Nancy now? Is she happier than when – you know – a few months ago, when she first took a break from work?

Marcus laughs.

I don't know whether to laugh at your candour or be offended by it. Ah, you know. It's tough, but she's a strong woman.

Any more clichéd platitudes up your sleeve? Shiv asks. How about saying she's a rock, a diamond geezer, a tough old bull? Because it's a bit of a front all that, the stiff upper lip, isn't it?

Shiv looks at him hard.

You're closest to her, Shiv says.

I am? Wow.

So, I was expecting a more honest answer. Look, we're mates, aren't we? No need for guardedness, secrets, no?

Marcus matches his smile with a snarl.

You had my wife, Marcus says. Is this your idea of fun? Getting pissed and goading me? What the hell is the time, anyway?

He listens for movement in the hall. Georgia's clipped and well-enunciated telephone voice can be heard through the wall.

What's with the sickly concern? Marcus asks. Because I don't buy it.

Eh?

Why don't you ask her yourself? Take her out for dinner?

I didn't…

Because I've been thinking lately. And I wonder if part of the problem, for Nancy at least, is that people are forever talking about her. Surmising. You know what I – it's hard on her. This is a new for her. She's proud, *you* know that, the older sister, the one who's used to being admired.

Shiv coughs. There is a click of heels on the floorboards. The downstairs toilet flushes.

Look, I'm worried about her, Shiv says. Last week here in this kitchen, she seemed… well, lost. Like she wasn't even sure why she was here, and…

Nancy returns. Marcus thinks they must look the picture of perfect amity, sat nursing their empty glasses together. Georgia follows close behind. As Marcus stands to leave, Nancy smiles, a warm, inviting smile. Marcus looks at Shiv and back to Nancy again. He sees it in her face, the moistness in her eyes. Shiv is back in bed with her again. The sentimental look he can recognise anywhere.

Georgia goes to investigate the sound of a car horn outside. From the hall, she shouts in to tell them their taxi's here. Marcus thinks she sounds a touch too breezy.

Already? Nancy asks, pulling at her ponytail. But I haven't even finished my drink.

Marcus grabs her arm and drags her to the door.

Steady on Marcus, no need for that, Shiv says.

Steady on Shiv, no need for that, Marcus says. Now, fuck off.

At the door, Shiv offers a handshake but Marcus darts out of the door and watches Shiv hold Nancy so close it's as if he's breathing hot, lemon breath into her neck. Georgia is nowhere to be seen. In the taxi, he fastens his seatbelt. Nancy struggles with hers but he doesn't offer to help. They pull away.

Well, I'm right, aren't I? You can't argue with logic, the driver says. The Poles – God. But the Moroccans, I've not seen a sober one yet. Cash payers, all, never cards and…

Shouldn't you be concentrating on the road? Marcus asks.

Sleepily, Nancy nudges him. *Be nice* her look tells him. She rests her hand gently on his lap and pulls her cardigan tight around her. Lazily, she nestles into him but he stiffens at her touch.

I saw that look between you, he says, as you two were sitting there, a line excluding me, I'm certain of it. It was a special look, intimate. You were *communicating* to each other. I won't be fooled, he hisses. This is not the alcohol fizzing in my brain. I know what I saw with my own eyes.

The rest of the journey home is in silence.

Two, three times he tries, until at last he resorts to bashing the bottom of the door open with his foot. He manages, like the last time, to do so without damaging the bones in his feet.

When they're inside, hovering in the living room, carefully, soberly, she steps out of her stilettos to reveal baby pink nails, chipped on the toe. She joins him on the sofa. Marcus stares at the unlit fire.

What did you say, Scabby Toes?

I didn't say anything. We should light a cosy fire, you'd like that, she says. There's a chimney, we may as well use it. I could buy some logs and kinder like last year in that cottage in Wales, remember? You used to talk about it all the time, you loved it.

What?

Fuck you, Marcus.

Nancy stares ahead, her legs crossed, her hands resting on her lap. She wants to move, distract herself. She looks at him and then brushes his thigh with her fingertips, cautious, conciliatory. Marcus suspects she's testing the water with him, but he's not appeased, he's angry. Sitting forward now, he turns to her.

You still think about him?

Who?

You know damn well who I mean.

I'm not rising to this, Marcus.

Oh no?

She shakes her head and stares up at the light fittings.

He fancies you, that's obvious. So, how does that make you feel? You don't exactly discourage him, do you? Come to think of it, why is it you make so much effort to see them? Well?

He emits a low, hissing sound.

Come on now, she says gently, I thought you were more secure than that, Marcus.

She knots her fingers together, as a signal she won't be touching him again as long as he carries on with his line of enquiry.

I need to know, do you think about him? The two of you together? His dark skin. Do you miss it?

He doesn't know why he's doing this, his head is pounding, but he feels compelled to eke a confession out of her somehow. Deep inside of himself, he's sure she harbours resentment towards him. He closes his eyes and listens to the tap dripping in the kitchen.

We went out and you left the taps on? She asks.

It wasn't me. If it was me, I'm turning into you, I'm turning into a lazy bitch.

I'm really surprised at you, she says. Why are you – how are you dredging this up yet again? I told you, I just need some more time, a few more weeks, that's all.

He stands and turns his back on her.

I saw you. The both of you. And they betrayed us.

They didn't – look, I doubt it was Shiv's idea, all this. It's mostly women who instigate these things, isn't it? I mean, it was me who brought up the subject of IVF that time. If it was up to you we never would have even had that conversation. But I didn't want to put us through that. All the mind-fucking tedium of it all. All that passive crap. We made the decision *together* to have a different type of life, a good life.

Gently, he turns around.

Don't try to be clever, changing the subject. You haven't answered my question. Do you think about him at all? The two of you together?

I'm not standing for this, Marcus. You're out of line. It's borderline abusive.

He snorts at this.

I'm having enough problems here, she says. I'm just trying to keep accord with my family. Cut me some slack for once. It's not easy.

He watches her rise up and when she reaches the door, she turns around.

He's with my sister! I let him go to my sister. I didn't want him, I wanted you. No comparison. You were smart and beautiful and everything I – when you walked in the pub, I couldn't get my head to think straight. The tiny squares on your jacket.

The what on my what?

Her face feels hot.

This is not just your problem, Marcus. If you think I'm looking at him like – as the one that got away – well, that's ridiculous. I can't – now this is – you're accusing me of looking for a lover indiscriminately.

The saddle feels small and needling. The cold air slices through him, but he's relieved to see the cul-de-sac is quiet at this time. From nowhere, a couple with their arms locked tightly around each other step out into the road. He slams his palm on his bell. The man yells at him for not turning on his lights. Carefully, he mounts the pavement instead, but in the next dip of the curb, he crashes back down onto the tarmac. Heading towards Brompton Cemetery, he rides faster than he does in daylight.

Earlier, he'd been desperate to get out of the house, burn some fat and some anger away. The girl's parents had been in his mind constantly and they wouldn't disappear, despite all his efforts. By contrast the girl's parents weren't angry. They hadn't lashed out or blamed. The downcast eyes on her mother, as if drawn on, as if a kid had been instructed to sketch a picture of grief in one of those new art therapy sessions, had pierced him. He watched her warm her hand on the coffee cup. The shadow of her ring finger quivered against the white polystyrene.

In great detail, he'd explained the risks for this type of operation. He'd told them problems can and sometimes do arise, it was nobody's fault. All the time, he could feel himself sweating. The tube, he'd told them, specifically the breathing tube, was positioned so it would be – but no, it was not his fault. He'd merely given them a line of self-protecting lies. A life gone forever. He was a liar, unconvincing, but it all happened so fast and he had to meet with them so soon after. No time to think. Her plump face had been stricken. But the father's face was worse. Not much older than himself. A couple of years, maybe. Early forties, maybe.

Grimacing now against the wind, he veers left to avoid a passing lorry. When he arrives at the gate of the cemetery, he slows. And his face had a broken expression. That crumpled nose of his and his sad mouth had not asked the obvious question: how did this happen? Instead in a quiet voice he'd asked how could this happen to them? She was only fourteen, a baby. She could have survived the operation, gotten better, beaten her cancer. People did it all the time.

He flies up out of his seat. Grabbing his mobile from the coffee table, he grins at her. He scrolls down until he finds Shiv's number. With his phone tight to his ear, he keeps his eyes firmly fixed on her.

What are you *doing*?

I have to know. Wait. Wait for it. Oh, here he is. Shiv, Shiv, can you hear me, mate? I'm after needing you to settle a little argument here. Yeah I know it's late and no I don't, but I won't – tell me, do you still fancy my wife?

I can't believe an intelligent man is doing this, she says. What are you, some kind of Neanderthal now?

He can hear Georgia's tired voice firing questions in the background. *Who's calling at this bloody time? What do they want?* Nancy shoots over and grabs the phone from him. She runs from the room. In the bathroom, she dangles the phone above the open toilet seat.

I was only asking, he says.

You weren't, you were goading him.

Christ, he says, come on now, not another phone. I'm still paying for the last one.

With her right hand gripping the flush, she scowls at him.

Would you like me to do this? I will, I'll flush it away. If you try and call him again tonight, I will.

Chris slaps his back so hard a quarter of his pint spills across the mistletoe and holly table display.

Thanks, Marcus says.

You're welcome. Be right back, I'm making mine a double.

Chris is early. Marcus was hoping for some quiet time to make sense of his thoughts. After lunch at home alone – Nancy had been out but he had no idea where – he'd headed into town to attempt his Christmas shopping. It hadn't taken him long. This year, he only had Nancy to buy for, which he figured was just as well as he wasn't in the mood. Town had disgusted him. The shops had been bloated with the stench of dirty money and cheap perfume. He couldn't stand it.

Emerging from Fortnum's in the rain, all he could think of was the girl's parents' faces, hurt, confused, disappointed and all because of him. Even the carol singers outside the Royal Academy had left him feeling dead inside.

He missed the wards at Christmas. He hadn't realised then, hadn't stopped to think, but even at Easter time he enjoyed seeing them arrange a quick round of hot cross buns for the adults, cheap eggs for the kids. It was something.

Chris slams his double scotch down on the table. Pulling his trousers up tight around his groin, he grins.

So, what's the craic, then? Chris asks. Tell me, what's the big emergency?

He takes the pint from Chris's hand.

Later, they'll all be arriving, Marcus says, the usual suspects. Shiv and Georgia, Anna and her strange little daughter – what's her name, Leonora? Nancy will have bought the turkey and cranberry sauce. No doubt she'll have Julia shadowing her as she gets it all ready. Where else would she be? And she's a whole day early! Christ, Merry Christmas. So, the tall and short of it is I needed to get away and you were the best option for such a diversion. Truthfully, the only option.

Thanks.

Chris settles down. Spreading his legs wide, he leans back.

You've got a houseful this time? Rather you than me, Marcus.

And what are *your* plans? Marcus asks.

Just me this year.

Oh, so what are you going to do?

I'm going to start the morning by peeling off my socks. Will have been wearing them overnight to keep my feet soft. Then I'll wash my hair, indulge in a little hot oil treatment. Maybe follow with a manicure. A dab of coral polish.

Marcus smiles to hear his panto-dame voice.

Then I thought I'd cap it all off with a glass of Malibu and fall asleep in my clothes.

And what'll you really be doing?

Chris leans forward and downs his double.

I've got a Fray and Bentos in and some Newcastle Brown Ale. I've got a week's worth of Sri Lankan cricket burned, and I'm just going to sit there and work my way through it all.

You lucky bastard.

Marcus looks over the top of Chris's head to the bar. The woman behind the counter glances at them both. Taking a tea-towel, she rubs a pint glass a little too diligently. He remembers the last time. Chris had tried to ingratiate himself with her in the usual alarming fashion. Flashing his teeth, he'd leaned across the bar breathing her name into her blouse. Marcus watches her fold the tea towels into a neat pile. Slowly, Chris turns in his chair and waves to her. She turns her back and refills the optics. Marcus feels a hand grip his knee.

William misses you, Chris says. I saw him earlier. It was the strangest thing: he seemed lost, like he's lost his fight. And he was so quiet in theatre earlier.

Is that so?

So, you've got a houseful tomorrow?

Just thinking about it makes me want to drown my sorrows, Marcus says. Five-Six-Seven in total. Or eight if you're interested in joining us? Can I tempt you over for a few hours?

Chris shakes his head.

Not me. Your parents going?

No room. We've got Julia and her numerous suitcases in the spare room as it is. The truth? I haven't asked them, too embarrassed. Shelagh, my mother, would be mortified.

About what? Ah, I see, I take it they don't know?

No, Sir. They think I'm working all over Christmas.

Nice. Is there a reason why you haven't told them?

And say what, exactly? Oh, you know Da, sending texts on the job. The usual. And yeah, the bum luck is someone actually died while I was doing it. I know, what are the chances? Still, we have a cupboard full of booze to offer you. I haven't drunk it all – yet. And look here: I've got your favourite whisky in. The one with the stag on the front. Let's down it together, yes? And my father who's never put a foot wrong. A man, who for over fifty years got up at 6am every day without complaining. Up before the sun to supervise those lazy bastards on the shop floor. The only time I heard him bad-mouth a colleague was when some dope-head ran over his foot with a forklift. He was on crutches for a week.

For a second he considers asking Chris about Asabi, but manages to stop himself. Chris announces he's going to the loo and takes his drink with him.

He wants to see Asabi. It scares him how much. There is too much that has been unsaid between them. What he wants is to understand her better. There were depths to her that intrigued him. Chris returns and settles back in his chair, glancing over at the barmaid, nowhere to be seen.

Do you all get on okay together? Chris asks. Any other chaps to play with?

Only Shiv.

Shiv? Much in common there?

Shiv. He's been feeling it in his jaw of late, neuralgia, he suspects, a result of grinding his teeth in his sleep. Chris taps his arm.

So?

Shiv used to fuck my wife, Marcus says. And if you ask me, he'd like to do it again.

What, they used to...

Yeah.

You've never...

Yeah, well I wouldn't would I – too busy. But now, too much time. I'm just churning things over in my under-stimulated head. Over and over and over. Never mind all that. Have you brought what I asked you for?

Chris slides over two synthetic morphine pills. The barmaid glances over. This time Chris winks at her. She empties a bag of coins into the till.

Is that all you got?

I'm not getting in trouble over this, Marcus. Just take it or leave it.

Furtively Marcus slides them in his pocket. Chris drums his fingers on the table.

So this Shiv fella. Go on, what's the story, did he dump Nancy?

No, I don't believe so. I think she wanted it to end. But that was then, and this is – look, to cut a long story short, he's having a baby – with Nancy's sister.

Okay, alright, complicated.

I don't want to tell you, Marcus says. I would prefer to keep it simple and light between us. You'd spread it all over the hospital in a heartbeat.

Chris slouches back, for once at a loss for a topic of conversation. Marcus smiles.

Okay, Chris concedes, let's change the subject.

What do you think of feminism, Chris? Do you think it's dead in the water, or is there more of a need for it than ever? Come on, feminism?

I think there's a reason for it from time to time. In moderation.

Okay, Marcus says. Not bad. Okay.

So, what's this all about?

I'm merely interested in your opinion. So?

If you hammer everyone on the head too much about it, Chris says, you'll get a backlash. People will lose patience with it. Same thing happens if you take quotas too far. It causes resentment. But to tell you the truth, I think a lot of people think feminism's redundant. They covered a lot in the Seventies, didn't they? Take pay. Now it's the same for everyone and…

Marcus grins.

And you were doing so well, Marcus says. Men still earn more than women. They're more represented in parliament, don't have the glass ceiling to contend with. I could go on.

Look, Chris says, there's fun in the backlash, isn't there? There's more power to their elbow. It's fun to get incensed by being hard done by now and again, don't you think? Don't you need that from time to time? A bit of fire?

The rain can be heard against the windows, the brickwork, the pavements. He wants to escape out in the grey-wet and cycle until his head bleeds. What he needs is to feel something – anything, even if it's just the battering rain and hail bruising his skin.

The silver ones with fish tails for handles weren't my choice, Nancy says. Just in case you were wondering.

So, they're Marcus's choice? Julia asks. Well, he will insist on the best, I've always thought so.

It's not Marcus, it's his mother, Shelagh. They were a present from her. He hates them every bit as much as I do.

Nancy brushes past her mother, dusts off the ice tongs and scrabbles around in the drawer for the cheese knife. She sees for the first time that some of the knives are broken with missing handles. Julia's hand gently rubs her back.

Someone's out to impress. Don't be going to any special effort on my behalf. Because I'll take you as I find you.

Everything comes back to you, doesn't it, Mum?

What do you mean?

Oh, forget it, nothing.

Julia carries the side plates out of the kitchen. Marcus wanders in dazed and empty-handed.

I'm tired of painting on a face, she whispers to him. I want to be alone, the two of us, a brandy and a DVD.

Let me help you with those, he says.

She hands him the cutlery and follows him into the living room. From the door, she watches him carefully lay the table.

Georgia heaves herself forward in the armchair. Shiv tips out the contents of Monopoly on the table. Georgia reaches her hand across and grabs the small silver boot. Marcus grins at Georgia.

So, you're proud of that rugby ball under your t-shirt, are you? Careful now. Don't want to injure yourself.

Georgia leans back in her chair, clutching the silver boot. Nancy heads to the bay window and sits on the sofa.

I wanted the boot, Nancy says for Georgia to hear. I always have the boot.

Standing by the laptop, Anna supervises Leonora.

Please Leo, Anna says, not Adele again.

Prince, then? Nancy likes Sign of The Times, don't you?

Nancy smiles and nods. Julia taps her fingers together but her lips are terse.

How are you feeling without Frank and Shelagh here this year? Julia asks Marcus. They would have appreciated an invite, everyone together in the same room, wouldn't they? We could have found room.

Up against his intractable silence, Julia shrugs and picks a magazine from the coffee table.

Leonora gazes up at the breast-shaped lights.

What do you think happens in heaven, Nancy?

What do you mean? What do *you* think happens?

Dancing.

What kind of dancing – jive, Argentinian tango, polka – what?

I'd dance when I'm a spirit, when the time comes. Do nothing else. Twist my body in odd shapes, light as tracing paper. Spinning like one of those windmills in the garden.

Leonora looks out at Blake's front lawn.

And I wouldn't get tired. Ever. I could move my limbs like this.

Nancy watches her spin around, skimming the pictures on the mantelpiece with the hem of her sleeve.

And what would you wear to dance in? Nancy asks.

A leotard, a purple one, like Madonna. High-heeled dancing shoes and red socks. But the music wouldn't be like we know it, it'll be different. It'd be kind of silent – but not.

Marcus, who has been watching them, raises his eyes to the ceiling. Coolly, Leonora seeing him, shrugs. Georgia calls them over to the table where the board is set ready. Nancy sits at the table. She takes another sip of wine and throws the dice. Old Kent Road.

I watched an interesting documentary on bullfighting last night, Julia says. Did you know they think Emperor Claudius brought bullfighting to Spain?

Georgia puffs out her cheeks.

Well, I thought it was – it was the kind of programme your father would have liked.

Leonora stretches out her arms again and spins in circles. Marcus mouths to Nancy words she can't understand. Anna relaxes into her third glass of wine. Oblivious to Leonora's spinning, she reads Shiv his penalty notice.

Nancy turns to Anna.

Sebastian, she says, has he bought Leonora anything this year?

Anna shakes her head.

Nancy can picture him stumbling through Hamleys, asking the sales assistants for advice to save himself the bother of thinking for himself. How could he know what she likes or doesn't like? An awkward lunch, fortnightly, over a pizza in Soho. Three scoops of her favourite ice-cream. Maybe a stroll around Hyde Park until it's bye bye, Princess.

You used to enjoy Christmas, she whispers to Marcus next to her, a break from all the drama at work.

She wishes Marcus was doing what he did last year, taking over the games, food, music. With his knuckles tense and blue, he cups his tumbler of whisky.

She glances again at Julia's sleepy face, leans across, takes the glass from her hand and places it carefully on a coaster. Lightly, she taps Julia on the shoulder. Shiv's black eyes meet hers. Together, they guide her out of the living room and into her room. Nancy touches his arm. It surprises her how much it makes her expand inside. He moves away, she thinks a little too quickly. He doesn't catch her eye.

This should be Marcus's job, not yours, she whispers. He's so bloody difficult.

I'll see if he's okay, Shiv says.

When he's gone she removes Julia's cardigan.

You go back in too, Julia says. I'll be fine here. I just want to think about him, that's all. Can't do that with so many people around.

I'm sorry, Nancy says, I didn't think. But I miss him too.

You know, he wasn't sure about Marcus in the beginning, Julia says, but he'd be proud of him now, all he's achieved and a consultant now.

I didn't know he had doubts about him.

Oh God, yes. Over-protective, probably. You know how he was.

Nancy kisses her on the cheek, leaves her to undress alone and quietly closes the door.

Marcus sits alone at the dining table, sprawls his arms across the surface and flicks the gold goblets still unwashed from dinner. Shiv pokes at the unlit logs on the fire and looks at him.

Stop that, Shiv says, it's annoying.

Marcus flicks them harder. The sound rings around the room.

Not man enough to get these going, eh? Shiv asks, sliding the poker back in the hook. He takes a seat opposite. They had soon tired of Monopoly. Marcus pushes his pack of playing cards into the centre of the table. Shiv shuffles.

Two cards for you, two cards for me, Shiv says. You know how much Nancy likes a real fire?

Marcus ignores this, Looking at his cards, Marcus resists a smile. Shiv turns his cards over. He flinches but then a slow grin takes over his face. Marcus's phone bleeps. He knows it's Asabi. Slyly, he glances at his phone. *Miss you*, it says simply.

Nancy enters with Georgia. Nancy perches on the arm of the chair next to her sister. He can't hear what Georgia's saying but he hears her tone. There's an air of mock-anxiety about her tale of all she has to do, all the preparations she has to make and how time is fast running out before the baby arrives. Nancy makes soothing noises at timely intervals. He glances past them to the television. Leonora wanders in, sulkily sipping a milkshake and sits cross-legged on the floor next to her mother, obscuring his view. Anna sends one text after another, but her sad eyes are glazed over and empty. Marcus stares down at his hand. He's only one card away from a pontoon, but he knows he can't risk taking another card. Shiv leans forward and slides five coins into the centre of the table. Slowly Marcus slides his share across, matching him.

I've got ten more, Shiv says, sliding ten more into the middle. Marcus ups him to twenty, and then when Shiv matches again, Marcus turns over a nine and his ace. Carefully, Shiv turns over his two cards, an ace and a king. Pointedly, he slides the pot over with his arm and tips the money into his wallet.

Well it is Christmas, Marcus says. I can do gracious failure at Christmas.

Admit it, Shiv says, you thought you'd won.

Well, maybe, yes but I was prepared to take the chance. I don't believe in playing safe.

146

Marcus hauls himself up out of the seat. He's tired now, but he has to get away. All seats in the room are taken. His head feels light and empty, but it's not a pleasant sensation, it feels to him like he has nothing to hold on to.

Another whisky? he asks Shiv.

Sure. Why not?

You can top my wine up, Nancy says from the armchair, handing him her empty glass. Leonora blows bubbles through a straw.

In the kitchen, he pours himself a measure and swallows it down. He pours himself another. And another. When he's back in the room, he hands Nancy her drink.

Marcus, there's bubbles in this.

You like a spritzer.

It's Christmas, Marcus.

He smiles at her. Back in the kitchen, he opens a fresh bottle of wine. He thinks of Asabi and reaches for his mobile. Her eyes, those limitless black pools, the bow of her back. He could make her day by calling her.

This pervading flatness was making him want to kick against something and he concluded, why not her? Mentally, she could match him; he met so few others who could these days. She seemed to be inviting drama. It would just take a little planning to play along.

When he's back in the room and sat at the table, he invites Georgia over.

I thought you'd never ask, Georgia says. I'd assumed I was

invisible. Here I am boring Nancy senseless with my baby talk.

Then come and play with us if you like, Marcus says with forced brightness, Nancy too.

Cautiously, Nancy pulls out a chair next to Shiv. Marcus deals the cards one at the time, slamming them down on the table. Nancy eyes him. He slides over half of his kitty to her. Shiv does the same for Georgia. Scooping the coins towards her with bony arms, Georgia sighs.

It is then Leonora slumps over, takes a coin, slides it around her palm for a moment and then spins it on the wooden surface. Shiv's face turns sour. He eyes Marcus, Leonora and Marcus again. Marcus notices what he's wearing for the first time, a Lacoste shirt with a few buttons undone. He smells of cheap, musky amber. Marcus slugs his whisky down.

Go easy, Nancy hisses.

Loosen up, he hisses back. You said yourself, it's Christmas.

Marcus shoots up and goes to the laptop. Seconds later Baby Please Come Home fills the room.

Georgia forces a smile for Nancy.

Leonora tires of spinning coins on the floorboards and rests her hand on Nancy's leg. Looking up from her phone, Anna smiles to see them all at the table. Marcus thinks Anna looks older tonight under the lamplight. He watches Georgia study her coins and she purses her slight lips. Georgia looks at him and quickly away. She circles the rim of her glass with her finger.

Where's Mum? Georgia asks.

In bed, Nancy says. Didn't you notice?

Dad's death must hang heavy on a day like this, Georgia says.

She told me she had a lovely time, Nancy says. She enjoyed today, considering.

Still, when the baby's born she'll have a new lease of life, won't she?

Georgia flips over her cards and reveals a seven and a nine. Still on the floor by the television, Anna stretches her arms up to the ceiling and yawns. Nancy turns over her cards.

Pontoon!

Nancy smiles and scoops up her pot.

Shiv smiles at Marcus.

Shouldn't you be going now, Marcus says to Shiv.

Already?

Already, he says.

Marcus, Nancy says, there's no need for that. It's still early.

But Marcus feels a rush in the back of his legs, rising up to the tip of his neck. His heart beats a thousand times a second.

Already, he says again, I want you all to get out of my house. All of you, just take your tedious wives and kids and just get the fuck, get the fuck out of my house!

Is there anything you'd like me to do, Nancy?

Um, no. Why would I?

You seem upset. Is anything the matter?

Julia gazes at her, sleepy-eyed in her dressing gown.

You're being weird again, Nancy snaps. No, I have it all covered. I always do. So sit back down with your coffee.

Obeying orders, Julia returns to her coffee at the kitchen table. She sits sadly stirring what's left in the cup with a teaspoon. Nancy silently curses the trains that won't run again until the 27th.

She has barely slept. When she woke at three, thirsty and angry, her anxiety had been such she'd felt like her head had left her body. It took her an hour of deep breathing on the sofa to feel her feet planted on the floor and herself again. Marcus, she assumed, had lay snoring in the bedroom throughout.

Julia herself might say, and probably had once, that she was too critical of Marcus, but what Julia couldn't know was she turned the criticism on herself more. Georgia joins them in the kitchen. From the large silver platter resting on the side, she takes a strip of carrot. Julia snatches it from her.

Now don't you – they're for later.

But I need my nutrients.

You're pregnant, remember, you're not ill.

Georgia had arrived early in the morning with Shiv. Neither of them had mentioned Marcus's outburst, but their unwillingness to acknowledge the incident unnerved Nancy and made her feel worse. As Georgia leaves, shaking her head, Julia turns her slippered feet towards Nancy.

It's been a while now. Have you thought any more about work?

Who, Marcus?

No you. I'm talking about you.

Nancy bristles at this.

It's Boxing Day, Mum, I've only just cleared away the Christmas wrapping from last night's presents, and already you're talking about work. One step at a time. Don't hassle me please, I'm working on it.

Nancy runs the tap and places a plate under. Julia grabs a tea towel and stands beside her.

Because it must be very odd having you both hanging around the house all day, Julia says. When your father retired, well that was a new one. It was a difficult time. You don't want that for yourself – not yet. Let's face it this is a strange set-up. I don't know how you stand it, young and full of energy. You must have so many plans ahead. Being under each other's feet all day, it's not natural. And Marcus always worked so hard. He must miss it – and…

Of course he does! He wants to get back. He wants to help people, do the right thing, he wants to be a doctor.

As Nancy's head spins, Georgia appears again, cupping her thin fingers around a mug, watching them both. Nancy is unnerved by her smile.

I don't know what I'd do if Shiv was around all day, Georgia says. I couldn't handle it.

He doesn't want to be at home, Nancy says.

And you're a great banker, Julia says.

Oh, so this is what it's all about, Nancy says. You hate that I'm not working.

You're too touchy, Julia whispers. You pretend to listen –

151

sometimes – but you always do exactly what you want to do. No wonder Marcus…

No wonder Marcus what?

Nancy stops washing up and stares out to the shed. Water runs into the sink until it reaches the rim. Julia turns off the tap. What she wouldn't give to be out in the shed.

No wonder Marcus what? She asks again.

Oh nothing. Forget I said anything.

If you must know, I've been thinking – about charities. I've found a human rights place in Shoreditch looking for volunteers. Maybe I could persuade them to give me an interview. I was thinking about emailing them.

She looks at Julia's face.

I want a complete change, Nancy continues. This charity in Shoreditch, they train you up to man the helplines, help with callers, basic legal advice. I want to do something that'll stretch me, make a difference.

Work work, boring, Georgia says. It's Boxing Day.

They take a tray each. In the living room, their opened presents are laid out around the tiles by the fireplace. Nancy looks at Georgia's pile. There is a set of oils in glass bottles from Shiv and a small envelope from Julia. Georgia sits and flicks through a magazine with a laughing baby on the front. Nancy looks away from her and out of the window. The low winter sun flashes in. Georgia blinks. Her palms rest on either side of her small bump. Julia moves closer to her.

Can I?

It's not kicking, if that's what you think, Georgia says.

I know, but I can feel the firmness where the fluid is. I love that.

She watches Julia's palms take the place of Georgia's, but there's no invitation forthcoming for Nancy.

Nancy sees two pairs of eyes blinking at her.

Nancy, are you listening? Julia asks. We were just saying…

Oh. Oh God. I should have put the joint in by now, Nancy says.

She returns to the kitchen. Pressing her hips against the edge of the sink, she stares out of the window to the shed, solid and faithful in the gloom. She heads into the hall, grabs the key from inside the box on the corner table and heads out. When she's safely outside she unlocks the shed door, enters, closes the door and closes her eyes.

You. You who followed me around, you who I resented. But I never complained to Mum, not once. Even as teenagers, when you were gawky, following me around, an embarrassment to me, and when I was married, I didn't want you to be bridesmaid, humiliate you like that, trussing you up in peach meringue. Christ, no, not ever, I thought of you, your feelings. The bitch sister and the one who…

She breathes in the varnished wood, opens her eyes and switches on her phone. Holding it up for some light, she scans the roof for cobwebs. There's one, glossy and silver. Slowly, she pats some warmth into her cheeks. From the darkness of the lawn, a small voice calls out.

Are you out here? Nancy, Nancy?

She watches from the dirty window. A strip of light from

the house stripes the turf. The crows stop their sound. The half-moon shines benevolently on Julia's white hair. Louder this time, her mother's voice calls out again.

Come on Nancy. We were going to play a game. Are you with us or not? Nancy, Nancy?

Not, she whispers to herself, not, not, not. Nancy looks at her for a long time; crazy, shouting into the darkness.

Nancy, Nancy?

They arrive late. Marcus grips a bottle of Sancerre in his hand, still smarting from earlier when they'd visited his parents' home in Kingston. As he'd handed Shelagh a bottle of pinot noir and chocolates for Frank, he'd been brisk. They hadn't reached the car before Marcus felt sick. It took him twenty minutes in the passenger seat to realise it was shame he was feeling, shame for abandoning them. No, no, can't stop, he'd told them. You know how it is, we're off to a party.

He unbuttons his blazer. The wind is a cold cloth around his chest. From where they stand on the step, they can hear the sound of laughter beyond the door. In the foreground is a muffled but deep boom. Sebastian, has to be.

Marcus studies the wine label and delicate, silver lettering.

Why didn't we bring the the cheap bottle? He asks Nancy. Anna just plies us with cheap, French lager anyway.

A navy pinstripe suit answers the door. The owner of the suit shakes their hand and introduces himself as one of the neighbours. When they're inside, the first thing they see is bodies laughing on the stairs. The air smells of spices and vanilla. Hesitating in the hall, they're unsure which room to enter first. Marcus doesn't want to enter any. The floorboards above them creak. They hear a door slam followed by a giggle.

Why is she hosting this damn party this year? He whispers. I thought she hated New Year.

She nudges him.

It's to mark twelve years since Sebastian left her, she hisses. She wants to show him she's doing just fine without him.

Looking at this picture book party scene, he says, anyone would think this was a normal family home.

Your caustic wit. Just don't push me tonight, please.

Sebastian takes their coats. She kisses Sebastian twice on each cheek. He moves in for a third kiss but she pulls back. He offers his hand to Marcus. Marcus grips it then quickly drops his hand. Sebastian throws their coats on the stairs.

In the living room, Leonora smiles, sucking orange juice through a straw. Nancy asks which room Anna's in and Leonora takes her hand, leading her out. When they're gone, Marcus wanders into the kitchen. Sebastian grabs his arm, cornering him by the fridge. Sebastian cranes his neck down to Marcus's height.

Anna says you've been off work for a while? Bit of an ordeal down at the morgue, was it?

Marcus takes a step back, apologising to the small woman he reverses into.

You might say...

Only, look, I'll cut to the chase, it's just I heard a little rumour? Not that Anna was gossiping, I might add, not her style, but I wheedled it out of her in that journalistic way of mine I'm prone to.

Marcus glances to his left. Following his gaze, Sebastian grabs an unattended bottle of vodka from the breakfast bar. He tops himself up, grabs a glass from the cupboard and pours one for Marcus.

Neat? That's how I like it too. Look Marcus, you know I like to keep abreast. Anyway, what's the deal now? You still a doctor?

Marcus wants to take a syringe and inject him with a sedative, but instead he calmly takes a sip of vodka.

What else do you know about me? My national insurance number? Do you know about that bout of thrush I had in the summer of 2007? I can hear a coke-ravaged voice from somewhere, was that voice coming from you? Yes, still a doctor, he says.

Because no offence, but it sounded like one hell of a mistake to make. Taking your eye off the ball like that. A woman, was it? Usually is. Super stressful that type of thing, I should know.

He inches near enough for Marcus to feel warm breath in his ear.

I should know, Sebastian says again.

Marcus looks past Sebastian to see a couple snogging by the back door. For a moment he misses Asabi so much he can feel it in his stomach.

Trust me, Marcus says. You don't want to get me started

on my problems. For one, we'd be here all night, and there's other people to meet here. For two, it's none of your damn fucking business.

Don't be like that, we're all friends together here, are we not? You've got to help out a poor soul, drowning in a sea of dull faces. C'mon, Marcus, fill me in, alright?

Enough about me. Marcus says sharply. I hear on the grapevine your new girlfriend's a bit on the mature side,

Meaning?

Meaning, she's twice your age.

Slowly, deliberately Sebastian smirks.

Not quite, pal, only ten years older. Actually, I find it all quite exciting.

Ah well, you know what gossip's like, like Chinese whispers, isn't it?

Who told you that, anyway – Anna?

No. Can't remember now. Shiv possibly.

Oh right, where is the virile bastard, anyway?

Sebastian scans the bodies in the kitchen, but there is no sign of him.

He's too good for the likes of us now, is he? Sebastian asks. Can't say I blame him. Between you and me I'd rather be anywhere else than here right now.

Artfully, he loosens a button on his linen shirt to reveal a smooth, tanned chest.

Because let's face it: Anna's friends aren't the oil paintings one would hope for, are they?

Marcus smiles.

I suspect this conversation could run and run, Marcus says, but must go, Nancy will need watering now, delicate little flower that she is.

He backs away, but stops at the silver tray to grab a glass of red for her. When he glances back at the fridge, he sees Sebastian is still stood alone. The others in the kitchen are happy to see him remain that way.

In the hall, he pulls out his mobile from his pocket, stops, hovers his finger over the letter A and types.

If you need any advice on how to fuck me over, then please don't hesitate to contact me. Please note that this deferral period does not extend or alter your statutory rights.

When he's alone again later, and Nancy's asleep, he'll call her.

Nancy feels a hand slip around her waist. Gratefully, she takes a glass from him. What she wants is to be at home drinking together. She remembers last year. A film, a confusing plot, something to do with time-travel, hard to recall and even harder to follow, but Nancy had loved curling up together until they fell asleep, just the two of them and the sound of Blake's party next door. They'd fallen in to bed just before Big Ben had chimed midnight.

He's restless, she can tell, and he leaves her to approach a couple by the window. He shakes the hand of a woman in a grey blazer. She reminds herself it's only a few weeks now until he returns to Bart's. She'd told Anna earlier he was desperate to go back. She hated to see his confidence sapped. It all happened so fast, this loosening of his grip.

Anna appears next to her. Nancy notices the stress lines in her forehead, and they exchange weak smiles as the volume rises around them. There is a loud bang and all heads sharply turn. The door crashes opens and Sebastian falls in, his grip firmly around the waist of a redhead.

That's Laura, Anna hisses in her ear. The mother of one of Leonora's friends. Look at her snow-wash jacket. Appalling. He can't help himself, can he?

Together, they watch them both giggling in the corner. Sebastian pulls at the bow of her neckline.

Okay, time everyone, Anna says. Everyone outside for the countdown.

On the lawn, they form a circle. Sebastian sidles next to Nancy, holding her hand with his left hand and Laura's with his right. A fine drizzle falls, obscuring Nancy's view of Anna's reaction. She feels the damp seeping through her suede shoes. There is no sign of Marcus. The moon is grainy and crescent and the air is strangely quiet as they wait for the chime of Big Ben. Suddenly, the blackness is pierced by a squeal. It sounds to her like a fox. Sebastian stumbles and steps on Nancy's foot. There is a hand on her back.

Sorry, Sebastian says. Don't mind me.

Not to worry, Nancy says. I didn't like these shoes anyway.

When it's over and everyone has filed back inside, Nancy grips Anna's thumb. In the living room with Marcus again, sirens whiz past like angry wasps.

Why did you invite him? She asks Anna. If he upsets you so much.

I wanted to show him I don't care any more, but then I decided he just wasn't worth the bother. It's Leo though, you know how she is. She wanted him here. Well, he is her father. Are Georgia and Shiv not coming tonight then? I did invite them. Yes, I'm sure I sent them a reminder.

Nancy feels Marcus's eyes on her as she sits with Anna on the sofa. He doesn't smile.

A little icy tonight, isn't he, Anna says. Why is he glaring at you like that?

This time, she has no idea what it is she's supposed to have done.

June beckons them across the waiting room. Together they follow her bloated ankles as she leads them up the narrow stairs. Inside her room, they sit on the usual foam chairs with only a narrow strip of carpet between them. June's eyes shine with expectation.

So how have we been?

Thanks for asking, Nancy says. We're a childless couple who've had the most staid, socially awkward Christmas ever, thanks for asking. And a terrible New Year too.

June switches her smiling eyes to serious and waits for one of them to speak. Nancy wants to tell June about the incident with Shiv, because it helped her to label it as an incident, nothing more than a stupid transgression, a moment of weakness, but instead she tells June about Georgia's pregnancy. She tells her about the smugness, the imagined disability.

June flinches at this.

This must be very difficult for the both of you, June says.

Why? Asks Marcus.

I wonder if you two have some regrets about your decision? June asks.

Oh yes, says Marcus. And what decision is this exactly?

Your decision not to have children?

We're totally fine with it, he says.

June's smile is cautious. The last time they spoke of this together, it had been decisive. Adoption had been an option but neither of them had wanted to put themselves through the ordeal. Last week, they'd both, without articulating it out loud over wine and dinner at home, had decided that neither really wanted to share their home with somebody else's child. But Nancy doesn't want to talk about this now. It dogs her, this intransigence, his unpredictable mood swings, another method of control, and he doesn't realise he's doing it. She feels her back stiffen, her head flutter. Still, she thinks, at least he's speaking this time.

And how do you feel about all this, Nancy?

She wants to say confused, missing Shiv, cut up and left for dead. Instead, she sits upright, crosses her legs and tries to order her thoughts.

I'm trying not to have a negative response to her happiness, Nancy says. Unlike Marcus, I'm trying my best not to take all this so personally.

Go on.

It's like we're both watching other people's lives unfold, but the two of us are stuck somewhere else. The only way I can describe it is it's like we're on the outside looking in.

She senses Marcus stiffen beside her.

We're on the outside looking into an inner circle, Nancy says. And this circle is full of smug families. That's how it feels. At least to me. More than anything I crave how we used to be.

And you? June says looking at Marcus. How do you feel?

Jesus. Why don't we get a pet monkey, if that's all this is about?

June smiles. You mentioned a holiday, once, have you thought any more about it?

Florence, Nancy says quickly. I'd like to go there. We're always saying we'll go sometime – why don't we? It's such a waste if we don't. We could could go exploring, no plans, just do it, walk and talk and stare at the hills. It seems as good an idea as any.

June tilts her head and smiles hopefully at Marcus.

And what do you think?

Marcus makes a low murmur noise. It sounds strange, she doesn't recognise it. Together, they wait and she feels like she's waiting for him to deliver a verdict on a disease.

A holiday though? I don't know if I can. Not now.

Nancy remembers in Barcelona five years ago, he'd huffed through passport control. Flying's no pleasure now, it's all wrong, he'd said. In the beautiful Miro gallery, glorious to her, he'd complained about the myriad steps they'd had to climb; the coffee had been too strong; the bright primary colours. A child could have done better. Queuing outside the Sagrada Famillia, his face had been an unrestrained scowl. Later that night, he'd suggested they go somewhere colder next time, but it was clear to her he didn't want a next time. She remembers the following morning, the silent, hungover breakfast in the Gaudi hotel.

June waits.

I don't see why I should suffer because of his selfishness, Nancy blurts. I have a right to a holiday, like anyone else.

What the hell? Marcus says. What am I supposed to have done now?

She swallows to feel her phone vibrate in her pocket. Shiv flashes through Nancy's mind but she pushes him down. For a second, she wonders if it's Tom, if she'll see him again. Was that meeting in the park his parting shot to her? Or will he want to hear from her again? If little Nancy had lived, would he think of her every time her name was called?

June coughs, drawing her back.

What happened at work, Marcus? Do you want to talk about it?

Well there was a botched operation, he says. But no, absolutely can't talk about it.

Can't or won't? June asks. Botched is an interesting choice of word.

Meaning? I hope you're not implying I'm taking all this lightly.

Not at all, June says, without offering clarification.

Nancy stares up at the clock on the wall. She knows counselling helps, even if Marcus doesn't see it, helped to talk, to be in the same room together with the soothing presence of June.

We're loners now, she tells, June. Cast adrift. No map for this, is there?

You say loner, June says. But there is another way to look at it.

Oh really? Marcus says. I can't wait to hear this.

June shrinks at this.

You say loner, you're both loners. But how about saying self-sufficient?

Marcus grins. Nancy suspects June is fearful of Marcus, and she doesn't blame her, a therapist advising a consultant doctor must feel intimidating.

Nancy doesn't know what they'll do now, how they'll fill the rest of the day. She picks up her red wool and wooden needles for the arm of the chair. She pulls out the needles and then stabs them back into the ball of wool.

Marcus looks wearily at her. He could go back to his research notes. He slams his laptop shut and turns to her.

Why are you looking at me like that?

I was just thinking of something – the other night?

What about it?

The look you gave me at Anna's party. Why did you scowl at me like that?

I didn't scowl at you. Look, what is this?

She can tell by the way he averts his eyes he knows her meaning. She waits.

When Anna told you Shiv wasn't coming – it was so – your face fell. It was so obvious. At one point I saw you scrolling down your phone.

So what if I was looking at my phone? Everyone does that. What the hell is that supposed to indicate?

You *wanted* to hear from him.

She wants to plead, enough of this now. Instead, she takes a deep breath and lets out a low hum.

What are you doing? He asks.

What do you think I'm doing? I'm trying to blot you out.

Why?

I know where this is going.

Well, you started it.

What?

Pining after Shiv like that, I saw you. And the other night at his house. I saw the way you looked at each other.

This again? You don't know how you make me feel, Marcus. How just looking at you – looking at you move, your frown when you concentrate, mind on higher matters. The little things you do. I feel tight in here.

She punches her stomach and coughs.

I did…

But you don't deserve my… don't deserve any of this.

I didn't ask for the sentimental routine, he says. I just want you to explain yourself. Tell me what's going on because there's the door. You can get the hell out if you're lying to me.

And what about poor June?

We'll go, he says. If you mean the holiday, if that's what you want, I'll book the flights to Florence tonight.

Before you change your mind?

I'm the reliable one here, he says. I don't tell lies.

And he leans back, satisfied.

Waiting again, she mutters to herself. It seems lately as if she's always waiting. The traffic shoots down the King's Road. Nancy stands well back from the edge of the curb. School children, a mesh of red and grey uniforms, file past her as she waits outside Peter Jones. She tries once again to be patient with her sister, convince herself there could be any number of reasons why she's late, but as she watches her lazily approach, she knows there isn't one.

Looking around her, at anything and anybody other than her sister, Georgia swings a straw shopping bag. Marcus had hissed at her only last night, her bohemian touches are never anything less than pretentious.

Am I late? Georgia asks.

She kisses Nancy on both cheeks and moves in for another round but Nancy pushes her away.

Only a minute or two. No matter.

Georgia smiles, but only for a second.

So, here's the plan, Georgia says. I need a Moses basket,

seen one here I like. The sales assistant tipped me off to come back in January. Should be in the sales by now.

Inside, they make their way over to the lift. Georgia stops and pauses to run her hands over a pile of soft toys near the entrance. Poking them, lifting and throwing them back down, she mutters to herself. Swiftly, she stuffs a teddy bear in her basket and walks on. Nancy follows her, remembering Marcus's words last night: *You know she'll be dragging you around, making you tag along behind. I'm surprised she hasn't arranged a little trip over to the Museum of Childhood in Bethnal Green to coo over the dolls houses too. Doesn't she have any friends to take? Or has she scared them all off for good?*

He'd spat his words at her. Nancy pushes the lift button and they travel up to the first floor.

They have adorable baby toiletries there, Georgia says. The really great thing is you can use them on yourself too.

The lift doors open, and Georgia's small frame, drowned in an over-sized Parka, steps out. Her birdlike, hunting eyes scan the shop floor. Nancy watches her dirty trainers pad the floor over to the baby section where she runs her fingers over a Moses basket – *Julia. Why didn't she rope her into going? That would have been more appropriate, surely? But no, Julia couldn't get away quick enough. As soon as the trains were running from Paddington.*

Ah, thank God, Georgia says. This is the one. What do you think?

Georgia folds it under her arms and looks around her. Fractious now, she begins rooting through the blankets.

167

The floral blanket, Georgia says. There's a matching blanket for it but I can't see it. I don't believe it's not here. But the sales woman told me…

Never mind. This one has lemon flowers.

Nancy hands her a blanket with flowers along the hem.

Lemon's handy if you don't know what sex it'll be, Nancy says.

No. I wanted…

But you can't magic it out of thin air if it isn't here.

Georgia's face whitens. She sucks in a sharp intake of breath, creases forward, her hair flopping down over her face, clasping her stomach.

Jesus, Nancy says. Help. What is it? This can't be right.

They both scan the room for help.

Shall I call an ambulance? Nancy asks.

Yes, now, I mean it. What are you waiting for? Now!

A sales assistant, all sharp fringe and heavy eyeliner in a navy blue shirt dress, rushes over.

Come and sit over here with me, love. Your friend will call them. It'll be okay.

That's not my friend, Georgia says settling down on a chair. That's my sister.

The woman pulls over two chairs. She sits beside Georgia, hugs her to her and Georgia leans into her matronly arms with frightened eyes. Nancy dials 999. Marcus always complained about neurotic time-wasters. No, Nancy tells herself, this different.

Georgia points down to the grimy untied laces of her right

trainer. The sales assistant ties it for her. From nowhere, the paramedics arrive and take over.

Don't worry love, one says. We'll take care of you. We'll see you're alright. Is your sister coming with you? Plenty of room. Careful now. Don't worry about a thing. No, you did the right thing calling us. Of course you did. Okay now?

When they're in the ambulance, Georgia lies back under a red blanket while Nancy calls Shiv. He answers immediately. She calls Marcus, and listens to his calm words beating into her ear.

As they hurtle west towards the hospital, she tries Julia's mobile again but there's no answer. She leaves a message, careful to report the facts, no more.

She peers in the Perspex incubator next to Georgia's bed. Web-like, the baby's fingers and toes are barely formed; her eyes are a smear of blue paste. Twisting like tentacles, the tubes keeping it alive look more harmful than helpful. She could be cradled inside the palm of her hand like a tiny, beached fish she's so small. Georgia invites her to reach in and touch her.

She can't bring herself to, in fear she'll break. Instead she throws her hands in her pockets. It shocks her, numbs her, makes her light-headed. She can't remember feeling so useless. Earlier at home in Fulham, Marcus had told her the worst case scenario. If she survives, there could be long-term difficulties, a likelihood of brain damage, or worse. Almost all survivors suffer damage in one way or another.

Julia returns with coffees, her face grey with the strain.

I just had a text, Nancy says. Marcus, he's given Shiv a whisky. He's talking him through it all.

She couldn't imagine the two together, how much Shiv will need him, desperately eking advice out of him, searching his face for reassurance.

Georgia closes her thin lips together tight and closes her eyes.

You look exhausted, Julia says. Try to blot us out, you sleep if you want.

This isn't what I ever thought could happen, Georgia says.

Nancy looks at the fish baby. They all do.

She'll be alright, won't she? Georgia asks. I just can't believe it. Why us? What the hell have we done to deserve this? What has the baby done to deserve this?

Nancy feels waves of helplessness starting again. She takes a deep breath in and holds it. Julia starts to cry. As she snakes her arm around Julia, she wants to curl up in a ball and cry herself.

Nancy looks at the baby lying in a half-world – a half-world between the womb that spat her out and the incubator creaking under the responsibility of keeping her alive. With the ward quieter now, she gazes out of a spotless window. Bare branches from the oak tree in the courtyard crease the sky. This is terrible, Julia whispers. This is supposed to be the most exciting time in her life.

The doctors are so good here, Nancy says. Marcus says so

too. You have to remember we're lucky to be in London at a time like this.

He admires the upholstered stool tucked under the dressing table, its ivory legs, bow-shaped and long.

The shower's powerful and clean, he says. Sink a decent size. You know, in the big hotels they have to clean the rooms in double quick time, otherwise they have their wages docked. Imagine having to peel used condoms off the ceilings and cum stains off the walls? Brutal. Inhuman. Are you going to stare at your face in the mirror all night? Did you hear what I just said? Have you read any Orwell? Hotels? Pretentious. And exploitative to the under-waged staff who work in them.

Yes.

Marcus falls back onto the bed and stares up at the cracked plaster above him.

For a budget room, it's fine, she considers saying, but she doesn't. She wants to avoid another discussion that at best will cause him to sulk, and at worst will risk making him angry. But she's stung she's had to compromise. She'd wanted to splash out on one of the expensive hotels overlooking the Ponte Vecchio. Browsing online, it was the tanned young women wandering around in Prada shades with silky hair that had sold her to the glamour. Nothing wrong with a *pensione*, he'd told her as he was booking it online. And you have the personal touch.

She'd compromised over the flight too, agreeing to fly a

budget airline she hated from past experience in the belief
they would at least be able to eat in the best places once
they arrived. Chris had sold him the idea of the place he'd
stayed once before with his ex-wife. He'd told him about the
old lift and the Virgin Mary hanging in the long dark hall.
There was a small terrace where you could breakfast facing
the cypress trees.

Checking in at reception had made her back stiffen, her
head empty. The receptionist hadn't understood her attempts
at phrasebook Italian. Marcus found it charming. Of course
you would, she'd hissed at him.

Their first breakfast had been appalling, he was happy to
concede that at least. There had been stale bread with tiny
portions of jam in plastic trays and biscuits that disappeared
on her tongue before she had a chance to taste. Really, worse
than none at all, he'd told her. But look at the view, she'd
reasoned. March, and barely even jumper weather.

From the bed, he peers over the top of his medical journal
and watches her dress. He looks at her curiously and places
the journal on the chipped bedside table.

Why are you still deciding? That dress looks fine as it is –
and I – well – I need a drink.

Can you give me a hand?

He leans forward and hooks her bra.

And this?

Fastening her Tiffany necklace, the one Julia had bought
her for her thirtieth birthday, almost ten years ago, the chain
is tighter around her neck.

This silver, how come it's still so shiny? Do you soak it in gin?

She twists around to face him. He thinks she looks glossy, healthier. Must be the air.

Ever the chemist, aren't you? It's just good quality, that's all. Julia only buys the best, you know that.

He remembers the jewellery he bought her in Laos, and he often wondered why she didn't wear the rainbow-coloured bangles and the ankle chain with bronze charms in London. She grabs his hand and cups it over her breast. A wicked grin, one that takes over the whole of her face. Playfully, he gives her breast a squeeze.

Nice, but I need to eat, he says.

I know you want more from me, she says.

She thrusts a cushion into his chest. Dust flies everywhere.

We're on holiday, he says.

I know! The pressure!

Look, hurry up, will you? I want to take a proper look around. Outside, red sky at night. Let's go.

On their way out they pass the man on reception who looks at them shyly and a line of solemn sacred hearts in the hallway. The lift shakes all the way down. They step out under a sky that matches his cerulean eyes. Shops are closing and linen tablecloths are laid on small, round iron tables. They cross the Ponte Vecchio under the darkening sky. At the far end, a woman with black, silk skin stares at them until they pass.

He thinks of Asabi.

He hadn't messaged her, yet last week she had texted him twice. Get in touch, she'd said, followed by two kisses in bold. This had worried him, he hadn't known what to say in response, if he should say anything at all. Only two nights ago he'd been awake all night at the thought of having to face her again – strange and volatile and hell-bent on mind games. The minions certainly have rights, he'd thought over and over, more than he seemed to, anyway.

He puts his arm around Nancy.

I should have brought my jacket, she says. I don't really want to go back to the room. Can I have yours?

He peels off his hoody and hands it to her. They pass a row of tavernas and stop at one to peer inside.

This one I think, she says blankly.

Inside, they're seated on a table overlooking the river, brown and unending. Relaxing back in his chair, he smiles at the waitress and orders two drinks.

The alcohol will warm your through, he says. A couple of limoncellos? Shiv.

She reaches her hand forward and strokes his thumb.

Nice, he says. Flirting with me?

You know, for someone on a holiday from work, you should try to relax.

A holiday from…?

Honestly, all this business about cutting corners on flights and hotels and…

What? You call my time off a holiday? On half pay and with the shame of a major professional fall. The waitress brings the drinks and comes to take their order. Nancy sits back and cups her glass.

You're not smiling, he says, why? Look at me. Look at me. That's better. Distrust in your face already.

He glances at the table next to them. Two girls sit with lemon bows in their hair, one small, one tall, both dark. As he drinks, he tries to push Asabi away.

What's so funny? He asks.

Nothing. Just the limits people place on themselves.

She leans forward and begins to stroke his thumb again.

Where were you that night? He asks.

What night?

You said you were at Georgia's. Only I just can't join the dots.

That night last year? I was at Georgia's. I took the long way home, that's all. Cleared my head of all the – I enjoyed it, as it happens. Much needed time to think.

Gripping your fork tight now, aren't you? Certainly. And the flicker in your eyes just then, contrition?

She smiles at him across the table.

Maybe, she says. Is that the right answer? Is that what you want to hear?

You don't normally go walking late by yourself.

Why do you ask?

Ah, he says. I wondered, that's all.

You're suspicious *still*? Us here together like this?

Ah, that pronounced swallow, he says. A tap of your middle finger on the knife. Too rapid, too nervy.

175

The waitress takes their food order.

Your eyes are flickering in and out of concentration, he says. Easy. Ah, the posture, the chin forward, the back straight. Self-defence. Now, you're straining to think of anything to say.

I've come to a few conclusions about this, if you must know.

Slowly, she leans forward across the table. Her top slips down her arm.

That's a sexy bra, he says, must be new.

Do you want to know what? She asks.

He takes a sip and waits.

It's perfectly simple. This is all your problem, Marcus, it's all in your head. You know what you are?

Tell me, he says.

You're a masochist, that's what you are. Now drop it, okay?

He smiles at her.

Nice argument, he says. Masochistic, yes. The stock psycho-babble defence. Very good. But the love mark on your neck, I saw it. A tiny purple smudge. That's the type of thing Shiv would do, leave a mark, anything to tantalise. Play the slow reveal.

Just look at everyone, she says. Wonderful. We could be a scene from a Fellini film.

Could we? He asks. I wouldn't know. I've never seen any.

The queue outside the Uffizi stretches as far as the designer shops she'd earlier tried to coax him into. Instead, he'd turned his back on her and darted in the chemist for some anti-inflammatories to ease his stiff neck. He'd looked around the square at the waking, early morning scene: an empty phone shop, a small bakers, a line of cafés. The morning sun had bounced off the tiles. All around them were black coats with matching shades. He'd felt triumphant.

This queue is formidably long, he says. We're going to have to admit defeat and save the Uffizi for another time.

Yes, she says. I thought it would be quieter.

It's a world famous gallery, he says brusquely. It's going to busy.

Defeated, she looks down to his red trainers, bright against the pale paving. Her eyes survey left and right until she focuses on a café, one of many. Before she has a chance to say anything, he heads off there himself. She follows.

Earlier, instead of joining him on the terrace for another unmemorable breakfast, she'd stayed in bed and called Georgia. Shiv had answered. He sounded exhausted, but his voice had lost some of the strain from the last few days.

They drink their coffee in silence. Finally, he speaks.

I enjoyed last night, he says. Away from the drip-drip tedium of the last few months.

I liked the food, she says, the rich, truffle sauce.

As they turn a corner into a wide street, he stops to take in an old woman in black sweeping her step.

The brickwork, she says, pretty, isn't it? Pinks and yellows. Battenburg.

But around the next corner he frowns to see an orange monstrosity, a kind of sculpture.

As wide as our lovely house, she says.

Would you look at that – what is it, some kind of giant doughnut? Arrogant. Why have artists got to impose their vision on the rest of us like that?

Oh and what about architects? Buildings are designed by artists too.

That's different. Buildings at least have a purpose. People live in them, work in them, make love, fight and shit in them. But sculpture is the absolute worst. They think it will add something to a place, but it only takes away from the landscape. You know what I'd do if I were asked to design one?

She waits, sure he will tell her.

I'd have little holes in the ground pumping out fresh air. Nobody would even know it was there.

He jerks his palms upwards towards the slate roofs.

It's old and beautiful here, he says, and so some clown thinks up this. It's *violent*, that's what it is.

Don't you think violent is stretching it a bit?

Violent, he says again, loud and neon.

They carry on walking and soon the orange doughnut is behind them. He slides his arm around her, pulling her towards him. She rests her arm inside his hoody. Slowly, he raises his face to the sun, enjoying himself, she suspects.

Along the bank of the river, their pace slows in line with the other tourists. Marcus stops and leans against the wall.

The night before they left for Florence she'd been optimistic about the trip. It would be good to see him enjoying life outside of work. He worked too hard, achieved an incredible amount in a short space of time. His constant need for movement would be slowed under the leisurely sun.

Frank, she suspected was the reason behind his ambition, this need he had to please him, without fully realising why, or even that he did feel a need to please him. She knew he adored Frank, his working class roots and his fierce mind. Frank had scrimped to send him to private school. Marcus always seemed embarrassed by the fact. She wonders who even knew he'd been privately educated. It wasn't something she'd ever heard him mention.

Where do you think we can go from here? She asks suddenly, surprising herself.

He looks at her hard and she swallows.

Let's just sit for a while, he says and smiles at her. He reaches his out his arm and she goes to him.

You worry too much, he says. So don't.

A gull lands and shoots off again. He stares as it flies towards the hills on the other side of the water.

You can learn from the birds, he says. Birds don't mull over the petty stuff. Really, just a few technicalities of science separating us from the birds, the animals, the fish. A few mutations of DNA over time, that's all. All of us come from the sea.

She nestles in closer to him.

You shouldn't rise to Shiv's bait, she whispers. He knows how to play you, that's all.

He shrugs and breathes out long and slow.

Yeah, maybe.

Mad all this, she says. So wrong. The only feelings I have for Shiv now are caring, distant ones. Brotherly, actually, if you must know.

A girl passes with a pistachio ice-cream. Marcus returns her curious glance at a man in a hoody kicking his heels back against a wall. Playfully, Nancy taps his back. He grabs her hand. She smells the biscuity air, almost sweet, and different from London.

What if we lived here? She asks.

I thought you wanted to live in France, he says. An open-top car and coastal roads. A spotted headscarf, Dior glasses, smiling red lips, you driving. You know my licence is three years out of date. Churches, he says.

Pardon?

Chris told me there are some amazing churches around here. Shall we go find one?

She follows him, her gaze fixed on the steady, rhythmic movements of his trainers.

Sipping her instant coffee, Nancy enjoys a new feeling of calmness up her back and in the back of her head. From the tiny bathroom to her left comes the sound of thundering water. The flush goes, followed by the turn of the lock.

She'd be happy living like this, she'd wanted to tell him

last night. She'd not realised that cutting corners could be this much fun, this intimate. She'd wanted to ask him why money had been so important in their lives? They hardly saw each other, was the truth. Life was pure and money stains. None of it mattered.

She'd felt close to him after sex. Last year, in a particularly stressful stretch at work, during an internal enquiry into missing money, she had pushed him away from her. There had barely even been a look between them. For weeks it went on. The last thing she'd wanted was sex. She'd read that the end of intimacy could mark the end of a relationship. Last night she was determined he would be close to her again.

The street lights stream in through the window, showing up the fine lines on the back of her hands. Her hands, he said, mapped the truth. For a brief moment she'd thought of Tom but he'd soon faded.

There is a thumping sound as he struggles with the door, but she stays still. She smiles, slowly puts her cup down on the bedside table and goes to the door. The rattles and thumps continue. She yanks open the door. With his feet bare on the carpet, he pulls at the back of her jeans, his hands till warm from washing them. The bed is firm, it doesn't creak.

She puts a tablet in the machine and gazes out. The blackbirds form a neat line on top of the shed. Behind her in the kitchen, he creeps up and rests his mouth on her wet hair, breathing, kissing, breathing.

The flight had been smooth, as she wanted it to be, smooth

as the space between the back of his knee and the bottom of his thigh and she was happy to be flying back. For the most part, everything had worked out more or less just how she'd wanted it to.

Adoption could work for us, he said on the plane home. They liked couples like them, solvent and caring. But she'd thought him naïve and had told him so. This was not what they wanted, that hadn't changed. What I need is more time with you, she'd told him.

The blackbirds fly in a line off the shed. She watches them. The rain is so heavy now it creeps down the glass, glossing the pane. Suddenly, she is hemmed in. When she turns around, he's gone again.

Outside, she stands alone in the centre of the lawn. She waits, but he doesn't come, not even to the window. Alone in the shed, she enjoys the ancient smell of varnish.

When she wakes in the middle of the night, she is alone again. In their bed there is a space where Marcus should be. Slowly, she creeps through the door and into the spare room. Seeing him there with the duvet up to his chin and a glass of iced water next to the bed, she smiles. The computer buzzes in the corner and the curtains remain open. She returns to bed and stares up at the swirls in the ceiling.

She roles into the middle of the bed. Later, in the morning, he appears and stands at the door with a mug of tea in his hand. He places it down on the table by her side of the bed.

Belfast Child again? He asks.

She thumps the clock.

Frosty in there, he says. I think the radiator's broken.

He joins her in the bed. She thinks he seems smaller somehow. Under the covers, out of view, she is wearing his pyjama bottoms, and she wants to show them to him. Slowly, she folds the duvet down and pings the elastic waistband.

How do you feel now? She asks him.

What about?

Friday. Work.

He folds his arms behind his head and heads out of the door.

Nancy hovers by the curb. It's just after midday. Shoreditch is grimy and frosty, and it's a sudden, re-orientating slap on the back, a brutal contrast to the streets of Florence. As she looks across the road to the Boxpark, she notices a deli and its misshapen herb breads in the window.

That place wasn't there the last time, she says. Must be new.

Been a while, he says.

The number 8 bus chugs past them. The wheels slice through a puddle but the sound is soon drowned out by a rushing train.

Is that overground station new too? She asks. I like the orange colour. It's been a while.

Anna arrives with Leonora. She hands Leonora over so forcefully she trips up the curb and the contents of her bag spill out onto the pavement. Nancy stares down at a hand mirror, some face wipes and a soft packet of cigarettes. Anna mutters to herself as she scrambles them back in.

Sorry, guys, she says, breathless. A lovely holiday, yes? Thanks so much again. Just drop her off later if you don't mind. Appreciate this more than you know.

The three of them watch her run back over the road to the station. Leonora looks at Marcus, embarrassed to be offloaded again, but he doesn't return her smile. Adjusting the strap on his bag, he looks left, then right, and shoots off ahead towards the cinema. Leonora walks by Nancy's side, swinging her arms. Inside, they pay their money at the front desk.

What are we seeing? Nancy asks Marcus.

Some kind of animated thing with talking toothbrushes, he mutters. A bit young for you, but better than nothing.

Nancy takes her to the sweet desk. Poking her fist through the perspex, Leonora fills her paper bag with prawn foam and acid-green laces. Nancy takes one and slyly eats it, but the sugar makes her cough.

So, have you seen Sebastian lately? Marcus asks Leonora.

Nancy bristles at this.

Poor Leonora, Nancy whispers to him. This obsession you have with Sebastian. Be nice. Leave her alone to enjoy her afternoon.

Marcus shrugs. Nancy holds Leonora's sweets as she heads off to use the loo. She throws Marcus a look.

What am I supposed to have done now? I'm only making conversation.

It's all a bit sensitive. Anna. She told me Sebastian has a new girlfriend.

Oh. Well, who the hell would go out with him? How long will this one last? He doesn't value people, especially not women. You saw the way he was at the party, in front of Leonora too. No wonder she took herself off to bed.

Anna had told Nancy the new woman in Sebastian's life was Laura from the party, supposedly Anna's friend.

Too cruel for her, Nancy agrees. Some people just don't think at all.

Sebastian never takes me to the cinema, Leonora says as they walk along towards the screening room.

Really? Nancy asks.

He did once. Then, after in McDonald's he just moaned the whole way through our meal. He said he was sorry for falling asleep but it was just so boring. He said everything's too long these days. He told me in his days everything was ninety minutes and no more. I didn't know what he meant.

School kids file past her in high visibility jackets. She waits on the pavement outside the office where her interview is due to begin. Staring across the road and through the window of a small coffee shop, she thinks how different East London is to Fulham.

Earlier, Marcus had left for work as if no time had passed at all. The anguish of the past few months had fallen away for her as soon as he'd walked out of the door. For her at least there had been a sense of order restored, and a new surge of energy within the four walls.

She rings the buzzer again.

After he'd gone, she'd picked up the phone and made an appointment. They had tried to sound casual that someone with her experience would deem to lower themselves to their small charity. The voice down the line had warned her it was a tiny office above a shop with an errant boiler. Was she still interested? She's buzzed in.

To her right as she walks in, is an office without a door. Men with long hair recline in front of outdated desktop computers. There are dog-eared posters everywhere, bands she's never heard of. As she heads up the stairs, she falters for a moment. When she reaches the top, she struggles to breathe in the dusty air. A wiry man with an ashen face appears at the door to greet her.

Welcome. Welcome. Can I get you a tea? Water?

She thinks he must be seven feet tall. He bends down to shake her hand and his grip is so tight around her hand she fears her bones will crack. He shows her to a small room. Stacks of drug pamphlets are piled high in the corner. They look as if they are about to tumble. Slowly, she scans up and down, across and around.

This is all so different, she says.

Yeah, excuse the carpet, he says, pulled from a skip. Nobody would have chosen that colour. I'm Taryn. Take a seat.

His voice is slurred, like the effort of speaking was best

suited to other people. He leans back in his chair and props his feet up on the desk. She admires the place, a contrast to the polished wood and stiff-backed chairs of her former Clerkenwell office.

Nancy is moments from Anna's house. Waiting at the bus stop ahead of her, a girl with pink hair clutches a can of lager and throws her a look. Suddenly, she is aware of her Saville Row suit. She feels as over-dressed as she had done with Taryn.

Rain falls lightly and she runs the last few yards to Anna's door. She hovers her hand next to the bell, but instead of pressing it, presses her ear to the wood. She hears booms and murmurs. As she opens the steel letterbox to peer inside she sees Leonora sitting on the stairs with her head resting glumly in her hands. The sounds are clearer now. Sebastian's voice booms. She thinks it's strange that he would be here on a week day. She rings the bell and Leonora opens the door. Nancy smiles apologetically and Leonora hugs her.

Is everything okay? Nancy asks.

Mummy doesn't want Sebastian to come home. But I want him to.

The volume rises in the kitchen. Leonora raises her eyes up to the ceiling.

Should I go? Nancy asks.

No. Wait a second. I'll tell her you're here.

Nancy hovers in the hall and looks around her. Up the stair walls, there are school portraits alternated with seaside shots, all of Leonora. There are none of Sebastian with Leonora. Leonora grabs her hand. Together, they enter a silent kitchen where Anna sits at the table. Behind her, through the French doors with his back to them, Sebastian puffs on a cigarette. With moist, red eyes, Anna turns to her.

So? Anna asks.

Nancy thinks that's typical of her friend. Knee-deep in her own dramas, yet she's always asked after others first.

Fine. I got it. They said I could start on Wednesday.

Anna leaps up and hugs her.

And Marcus? He's back at work today, isn't he?

Weakly, Nancy smiles. It is then Sebastian turns around and waves at her through the glass.

A good actor, she whispers to Anna, anyone would think there hadn't just been a huge row in here.

That silly bitch he's taken off with, Anna hisses, fucking *Laura*. She wants him to move in with him. But no, too much like hard work for him, isn't it? So, you know what he wants? Yes, you guessed it.

But he has his own home, Nancy says. What about his bachelor pad in Fitzrovia?

Not any more, he doesn't. He's sold it and now he says he wants to go freelance. Of course he's being manipulative, says moving back in here is the best thing for Leonora.

Best thing for his wallet, Nancy says, I'm sorry, but it's true. What could be more unsettling for Leonora?

They hear the door slam. Sheepishly, he wanders in and

flicks his cigarette stub into the sink. Discretely, she looks at his long fingers, yellowing around the tips.

Nancy, he says. Good to see you. Hope all's well with you and the naughty doctor?

He grabs his jacket and shouts his goodbyes up to Leonora. The door clicks shut. Crying now, Anna tugs at Nancy's sleeve the way Leonora used to do.

Do you understand? Anna asks. It's too hard being alone after Mum died. All the things I have to think about and deal with.

From the kitchen, they hear Leonora's feet pounding down the stairs. She stomps into the kitchen changed back into her pyjamas. She hands Nancy her new ballet shoes.

Very nice indeed, Nancy says. I bet you dance better in those.

Satisfied they've been sufficiently cooed over, she disappears again.

This is her new thing, Anna says, but I told her tap would've been better. The weight of her, you know? You want to stay for some food?

Not today.

It was pretty grisly before you arrived. But you've really cheered us up. Especially Leo.

So, what will you do about Sebastian?

Anna shrugs at this but as Nancy steps out into the drizzle, she knows exactly what she'll do.

Marcus's stomach rumbles. Alone in the canteen before the

midday rush, he waits for her to draw near, hoping the rumble in his stomach will pipe down before she reaches him. She brushes her fingertips across his table, skin flawless under the strip lights, uniform crease-free.

Dr Connell, she says. I hope we can carry on being professional with each other after all this embarrassment.

There are tiny holes in her ears, and he thinks she must have had them pierced while he'd been away, he had been sure her ears were smooth. In his diary the night before he'd written: *Strange to think the level of attention I used to give her. That starched professionalism, assuming younger means polished and better. My fixation with her, why? I could teach her, that was all. While Nancy had been obsessed with herself, I just needed a pet project of my own. She knew what Nancy was going through. She's smart. No doubt she knew my unconscious motivations better than I knew them myself. For all your smartness, I like you. I enjoyed our game. So much so, I'd like to take you out for a drink and get to know you properly. But you wouldn't want that. You have friends your own age to meet after work, to gossip with about the monsters you works with, arrogant pricks like me. They'll be watching me closely, their eyes floating around the room.*

Of course. Why do you ask?

Well... you didn't look at me in the meeting earlier. I thought if we've got to work together...

For once he hopes she takes his half-smile as a warning. He doesn't hold on to it for long. With his pager on the table now, she leaves him and saunters out through the door.

Taking a tray, he approaches the serving woman with zeppelin arms.

Not much choice again today, she says to him. Soup?

He grabs a spoon and tests the salt levels. Later he will have a heart bypass to preside over.

In the pub after his shift, Chris waits for him. Upturning the contents of his wallet onto the table, Chris counts his collection of coins.

Must be nearly £1 in bronze here, Chris says.

What is it you're doing?

Linda's idea.

Linda?

Look, she's getting me into good habits. Linda says every penny counts. Take last night when she was cleaning my flat – I know, I know – she found five pounds behind my sofa and she said to me *you know that's a bottle of wine*. Because that's how she measures money, in terms of how much wine she can buy. I like that.

He slides the coins towards Marcus, as if to visually ballast his point.

And I have enough here for a couple of cans of lager. I'll put that in the metal tin she bought me tonight.

She bought you a tin?

For my birthday last week.

Chris sits back, satisfied.

Right, says Marcus. In that case, your round.

What, at these prices? Sorry mate, can only have the one. Cheaper to drink at home, Linda's idea.

Gingerly, the barmaid approaches to take their empty glasses, but this time Chris doesn't meet her eye. Confused, she retreats back to the bar. As she loads the dish washer, she glances back at them. Marcus detects some relief in her blank expression.

But you earn almost as much as me, Marcus says. There's no need for these tight-wad measures, surely?

Just trying to save some for a change. Actually, I'm getting high on it.

On what?

The frugality, the thrift, whatever you want to call it.

Chris scoops the coins back in his wallet. Did you see Asabi today? And did you see Will? He's gutted you're back. I'd be careful if I were you, he's sure to have something planned.

Linda, how did you meet? It all seems a bit sudden.

Well, we've been emailing each other for some time.

So you met online.

Yes.

I can see that, Marcus says. Someone as peculiar as you would thrive online. Easy to gloss over the quirks in your personality with a carefully photo-shopped avatar. With your mouth closed and your teeth out of view, you're certainly passable. In the right light, you could even seem appealing.

How the hell would I know? Chris asks.

So, was it love at first swipe?

Nope, at least not for me. Although I can't speak for her,

obviously. To tell you the truth, the first date went... well... she went all out to impress and I didn't like that so much.

But not *too* much. Honestly, for someone so undeserving, your confidence is dazzling.

And she kept trying to wheedle out of me how much I earned. She wasn't subtle about it, either – flicking her hair back and cocking her head to one side. When I told her, she curled her hair with her finger all girly. Well, it really rankled.

Shifting on his stool now, Chris looks around him. Marcus suspects he would prefer to be at home with Linda rather than out with him. Moreover, he still wasn't sure Chris had crossed the divide between being a colleague and friend. Despite his moments of kinship, he remained distant.

And how is the beautiful Nancy? And how was Italy?

Creamy pasta, fine wines, Ponte Vecchio. A lift that shot up and down in the dark. A dodgy shower. But you'd know all this yourself from way back. The rest though is strictly private.

Ah, well, Chris says, the important memories stay inside, as if by releasing them to the pigs they become slop.

When Chris is gone and he's alone again, he takes a moment to mull over the events of the past few days. Tearing strips from his coaster, he thinks of Nancy. He rises up out of his seat, the barmaid smiles at him, and he steps out into the rain. As he heads home he passes William's Bentley in the car park.

In Old Street, the air is cold. Nancy allows it to hum around her until she hums along with it. Last night in her diary she'd written: *I'm going to be fine now, everything's falling into place. This is a new turn of the wheel. Paula, though, my new colleague, she'll need longer, those skinny jeans, the feet on the desk, passing through my tiny room to use the toilet. She doesn't like me, I can tell. Probably resents a management change. But it's not a stretch to say they admire me. Earlier in the morning, everyone in the small team had fallen over themselves – nearly everyone. Trying his best to please me, to make sure I wasn't scared off by the mouse in the stock cupboard, Taryn had wandered in and out of my tiny office to check I had all I needed.*

Suddenly, she feels like running the last few yards to the deli. A few years ago, when she'd been in New York working for a month, she'd picked up a little trick. There, they'd pounded to the office in trainers and tucked their stilettos away in their handbags.

But nobody had asked her why she'd taken a drop down. She'd tumbled from the high echelons of the banking world and magically appeared in their rat-infested hole above a drug fanzine.

She checks her watch. She is five minutes late for lunch. When she arrives at the deli, Julia is already there by the window. Through the glass, Nancy watches her unfold and relax her arms but not her face. She heads inside and kisses Julia. Together they sit and gaze out onto the street. Nancy senses there's something on her mind.

Julia watches the crowds pass: a mess of artists, some skinny students, a platinum-haired punk. She cups her coffee tightly.

I can't believe all this, Julia says. They had it all so worked out, those two, so sensible.

But Nancy is irked by her simple summary of them.

Their life's not been so perfect. Nobody's has. Good yes, but perfect? Who does achieve that?

Julia's mouth hardens. Nancy thinks it can't be much fun dragging her ageing body around London. But something about Julia was unbreakable and resolute.

You've hardly touched your coffee, Nancy says. Something wrong with it?

Sliding her wedding ring up and down on her finger, Julia stares out. The minutes tick on until it's clear to Nancy she's not going to ask about her first day. She would like to tell her about the whispering coming from Taryn's office. The photocopier that conked out every time she pressed the button. Paula's pertinent eyes when she'd nervously asked her to send an email. Julia turns to her.

After all you've been through, Julia says, you know I'm – you've picked yourself up and started again. I wish I'd been strong enough to do the same. I'm sorry I haven't said it before, that I think that. I sometimes wish I'd been braver after your father died.

Nancy sees pain and regret in Julia's smile.

I regret not having spent more time with him when he was alive, Julia says, time with him alone, just walking and talking. Because contrary to what everyone says the best times weren't always the holidays, or the expensive meals out, they were the simple moments, the empty minutes that nobody wants to hear about, taking a walk together.

Nancy's hand taps hers, drawing her back.

What are you thinking about? Julia asks.

Do you remember that time in Greece with Dad?

Rhodes?

Yes. All of us were weak with sunstroke, remember? We walked along the seafront in one straight line. You, him, me and Georgia crying in her pushchair. The guy behind us, he was like – well, he was huffing and puffing at us. We took up the whole pavement, remember? Us as a family. And Dad turned around to him.

Oh yes?

Dad stopped walking, remember? The guy went crashing into the back of him and Dad spun around and spoke to him in Greek. A warning, a few lines, that's all. It was a bit of excitement, remember? A bit scary. We asked him what he'd said to the greasy man with the medallion, and we kept asking him, but he didn't want to tell us. We kept on and on and on until in the end he told us.

What did he say?

Everyone else can wait when I'm with my family, he said. Because I measure time differently to you.

Julia smiles and takes a sip of her cold coffee.

He said that? Oh yes, he did, didn't he? I remember now. Tomorrow, can I stay with you and Marcus? Maybe we can go to the hospital together.

Of course.

Then, pulling her khaki coat from the floor, Julia smiles. She pats her jean pockets, checking for her keys.

As he finishes his coffee, he wishes he'd brought back some Italian coffee from Florence, but there was no resurrecting the hills and clean air.

Slowly, he scrubs the coffee stain from his jeans and looks out of the window. Blake in a shirt and tie, bends down to weed his lawn. Blackbirds chirp on the toilet roof. He looks across the length of the lawn and the long grass zithers in the wind. He notes there are a few errant dandelions he will need to kill too.

Nancy calls to him from the hall. He goes to her.

Did you find the book for Shiv, and the grapes? Oh, and the champagne?

It's all here in the rucksack, he tells her.

As he forages around for his keys in the pot by the door, Julia approaches. Nancy buttons up her coat, red with large buttons, and opens the door. As she does so, he looks at his wife's face in the low, winter sun. He prefers the expanding lines around her eyes these days, they suited her, a kind of semaphore for it all.

He fetches his trainers, and they head off together.

At the hospital, he picks up Lily Ann in the way he has been trained to do. He cups her head in his palm and turns to face them all. Carefully, he hands her to Nancy. Holding her, she turns away from them to see a trolley being pushed slowly down the corridor. Nancy twists around and glances back at him for a second. Julia pretends to read and Georgia puts down her magazine and yawns.

Marcus takes the baby back. Her nappy is no bigger than a folded handkerchief. He studies the web of her toes that have started to recede. Her nostrils, though, are still no larger than the hook of a needle. He touches the downy hairs on her face and tiny milk bumps around her mouth.

After he's handed her back to Georgia, he sits down and flicks open his pager. He needs to tell them he has to go now. But he doesn't. Gradually, the room cools. A beam of light slices through the room, causing the baby to blink. The squeaking trolleys stop, the nurses disappear, and there's silence.

His pager vibrates once more and he turns it off. Nancy asks him if he's late already. As he heads into the warm light of the corridor, a nurse walks past him, smiling shyly, keeping her head down, afraid to look him in the eye and he is afraid too, for once of being witness to the power he has.

Acknowledgements

Thanks to Phil, Patricia, Mark and Matt.

ABOUT THE AUTHOR

Suzy Norman grew up in Monmouthshire then moved to London where she completed her MA at University College London. She is a freelance journalist, actor and fine artist. One of her paintings was on digital display at MOMA, New York in 2018. Her photography has appeared in *The Guardian* and at the Royal Academy. Patrician Press published her first novel, *Duff,* in 2015 and she has contributed to the *Refugees and Peacekeepers* and *Tempest* anthologies, also published by Patrician Press.

BV - #0035 - 040919 - C0 - 216/138/14 - PB - 9781999703042